COLLEGE SERIES

AbraXus Tasker College

XTC College Series

Ali Whippe

4 Horsemen
Publications, Inc.

Published By: 4 Horsemen Publications, Inc.

4 Horsemen Publications, Inc.
PO Box 417
Sylva, NC 28779
4horsemenpublications.com
info@4horsemenpublications.com

Cover by Autumn Skye
Typesetting by Valerie Willis

Library of Congress Control Number: 2022952158

Paperback ISBN-13: 978-1-64450-803-9
Audiobook ISBN-13: 978-1-64450-805-3
Ebook ISBN-13: 978-1-64450-804-6

AVAILABLE COURSES WITH XTC

OFFICE HOURS. 1

TUTORING CENTER. 57

ATHLETICS 97

EXTRA CREDIT. 137

ALI WHIPPE. 175

Office HOURS

Ali Whippe

Table of Contents

1		5
2		12
3		17
4		20
5		24
6		28
7		34
8		45

DEDICATION

To J, FOR THE NAUGHTY DREAM

1

$\mathcal{T}$he professor isn't in the habit of picking up strange men and bringing them home, but she's always willing to learn something new. A one-night stand is an experience she always wanted to have, and tonight seems like the perfect time. And he is perfect: dark hair just long enough to wind her fingers in, eyes with a hint of mischief, a mouth that looks like it was made for trouble. A body strong enough to lift her up when things get heated combined with long, delicate fingers that promise to find all the right places. Her skin shivers just from meeting his eyes across the room.

The stranger is dressed in a simple blue button-down shirt, top button opened at the collar to let him breathe, and loose khakis, his lanky form lounging casually against the wall near the bar. He nurses a drink, liquid amber in a small tumbler, remnants of melting ice cubes clinking along the bottom. He gestures at her with the glass when she meets his eyes, a look of pure invitation, desire in his dark eyes. She makes her way over to him slowly, careful of each step, not trying too hard to be sexy, focusing so that she doesn't trip and make a fool of herself. She's had a few drinks and it is starting to show.

The professor isn't particularly alluring. She isn't bad, of course, but a solid six out of ten. Her breasts are large, her ass is round, and her legs both work fine. Her face is acceptable, but she'll never see it looking back at her from a magazine. In the past, most of her relationships have been based on her brain. She's smart, clever, and sometimes funny. She's a fun-to-be-around, easy-going, casual flirt. She doesn't wear high heels or short skirts. She rarely wears makeup at all, though tonight she has splurged on some eyeliner—not that it is particularly visible behind her glasses. Her hair is short and simply cut, her body a little softer than it should be, but still perfectly functional. The few men she's had relationships with haven't complained, but they haven't written any sonnets praising the virtues of her form either.

She usually sticks with the chatting, a little flirting, some innuendos. She never pursues things after that. It always seems like too much effort. If she meets someone she wants to date, she'll want to get to know him first, talk with him and see who he is.

Not this time.

She doesn't particularly want to date the stranger near the bar.

She doesn't care about his childhood winters spent ice skating on the pond. She doesn't care about the novel he is inevitably going to write someday. She doesn't care about his car, or his condo, or his clothes.

Well, maybe his clothes.

Okay, she cares a lot about his clothes. That shirt and its buttons, those little plastic circles practically begging her to release them, pop them free one by one as she runs her hands down his chest. Would he be hairy? She takes another look, scanning those hands again, eyes ranging up his wrists. Maybe.

Her gaze finds his face again, and he is still watching her as she watches him. Her expression must tell him everything he wants to know. She's never had much of a poker face.

Steeling herself, she takes the last few steps toward him, her eyes boldly meeting his. She wants to say something sexy, something clever, but the words die in her throat. How does one normally begin? Introductions, of course. He will ask her name. She will reply and ask his.

But she doesn't want to know his name. She doesn't want to know anything except how it will feel to have those hands pressed against the small of her back, those lips hard against her own, her fingers twined in that dark mop of hair. She wonders if he will take his glasses off to fuck. He seems the type. She always keeps hers on. She's blind without them, and she likes to see what's going on.

They stare at each other, and she waits for him to speak. He doesn't. He just keeps looking at her, the same smolder kept just under wraps. She decides that she has to have him.

"Come with me." She had meant to ask it, to phrase it as a question, but it comes out as a command, and she lets it.

He nods and places the glass in his hand on an empty table. He takes her hand and lets her lead him through the warm bodies in the bar, hands a slow tentative connection of skin as they make their way around the other people. She likes how his fingers alternately press against her palm and twine between her fingers, sensitive skin responding to the different pressures.

She tries to think of where to bring him. The back room doesn't seem likely. She doesn't know this place well enough to know of a secret hidden room somewhere. The restroom will be filled with people, so that is out. She also isn't quite lost to lust enough to consider fucking in a dingy stall. Not tonight anyway. She has some standards, and comfort is one of them. Cleanliness is up there too. She sees the sign pointing to the restroom and turns the other direction, tugging him down a long hallway that leads to an exit door. Outside is a good start.

As they break through the door into the humid night air and hear it slam behind them, she turns back to face him, linked hands tugging him closer. He doesn't hesitate, pulling her into him for a kiss that is all promise of good things to come. She lets herself melt into him, reveling in the feel of his lips on hers, the warmth of his breath on her tongue. His hand presses against her face, holding her to him, and her fingers find their way into that hair, using it to pull him even closer. He groans as she tugs, and their feet stumble a bit, and then he is pressing her against the wall of the building, cold concrete blocks spreading a chill through her back.

He is strong, one arm reaching around to lift her up, hand firmly gripping the curve of her ass as they kiss, her legs wrapping themselves around his hips, excited to feel the hardness pressing against her. His mouth grows more insistent, and she is glad that she is wearing a skirt. His hand leaves her face and reaches down between her legs, fingers rubbing exactly where she wants them. He pushes aside the edge of her panties, and she shudders as his skin touched hers. She moans against his mouth, sucking on his upper lip as his fingers grow more insistent.

"Yes," she moans, pressing herself against him, needing that rhythm to continue, feeling the slow satisfying burn begin low in her belly. "God yes."

She shudders her release against his hand, his fingers pausing to let the moment shatter her, and she sags against him, lips still pressed against his. She feels him smile, and he kisses her again, tentative at first, wondering if she is done or wants more.

She is not done.

She opens her eyes and gives him a slow languid smile as her hands work their way to his belt. He lets her down slowly, letting her feet take the weight carefully as her legs wobble just a little. She unbuckles his belt with steady hands and bated breath, fingers quickly unbuttoning his pants and reaching within. She knows from the bulge pressing against her while they kissed that she will not be disappointed, but it is still a relief to find a sizable cock inside. She pushes him through the hole in his boxers so his pants won't fall down while they stand there, sure to caress every inch of him as she does so. He inhales sharply as she grips his shaft, hooded eyes watching her intently. His hands wander back to her hips, a question in his cocked eyebrow as he lifts her slowly, pulling her toward him as they lean against the wall. He presses the tip of his cock against her, and she pushes back against him, aching to feel the length inside of her, their skin separated by the thin fabric of her panties.

"Please," she moans against his lips as he presses closer into her, and then she is reaching down between them, fingers pushing her panties aside to allow him access. He bites her lip as he enters her, hands splaying beneath her ass as he presses himself inside. She kisses him hard as he pulls back, and then thrusts into her again. She uses the motion to push herself off the ground, rocking her hips back and wrapping her legs around his hips. His hands slide around to her sides, one running down to grip her thigh where it wraps around his hip, the other slipping up to grip her chin and hold her face close as they kiss, his hips pumping rhythmically against her, his cock stroking every inch of her, building and pulsing until she cries out against his lips, and he holds her steady as she shudders.

"Look at me," he orders, voice rough, and she opens her eyes to see him watching her as she comes on his cock, his face a study in desire. "Again," he demands, "Come again," and then he is fucking her again, harder and harder against the wall, and that pulsing brilliance is back in her belly, and she knows she is going to do as he commands.

"Yes!" she yells, but the word is lost in his mouth as he kisses her again, and she loses herself again to the rhythm, to the blinding need that drove her to go out in the first place. Finally, she thinks, finally! Good-God-fucking yes-finally! And then he is slowing down, waiting for her to come back to herself, and they meet one another there, in that perfect place of satisfaction, where it's enough, definitely enough, but there's also the chance for one more, just one more moment of ecstasy. He reads her mind, or her face, or her body, and kisses her again, slowly this time, letting the moment build as it will, their bodies entwined against the wall, all thoughts of anything else but one another forgotten. There is just his mouth, and her hands in his hair, and his hands on her warm skin, and his cock hard and throbbing inside her sliding sweetly back and forth, back and forth, and when she can't stand it anymore, she tugs his hair and makes him look at her. "Now," she commands him. "Come for me. Now."

His rhythm doesn't change, doesn't increase, but keeps on in a steady pulse, and she lets the orgasm shatter her as it does him, bodies shuddering together, and then they are slowly sliding down the wall, her ass landing in a soft thump on top of his thighs as he first kneels and then sits down on the ground. She wraps her legs around him and rests her face against his shoulder, breath ragged and heart pounding in her fingertips. His arms hold her tight against him, and she can feel his pulse pounding as they sit there.

When she finally looks up at him, heart slowed to a semi-normal rhythm, he is smiling down at her.

"Why hello there," she says, not knowing what else to say.

"Hello yourself," he replies, and then he kisses her again, mouth soft and gentle, the roughness of the previous moments gone but not forgotten. When they part, she looks at his hair, seeing how her desperate grip has pulled it in wild directions. She grins sheepishly as she reaches up to pat it back into place. He catches her hand as she pushes a lock behind his ear, and pulls it to his mouth, placing a delicate kiss on the back of her hand.

"Thanks," she said, not sure if she is responding to the hand kiss or the impromptu fuck.

"Any time," he replies. He moves his legs beneath her. "While this is lovely, I need to move."

"Oh!" she exclaims. "Sorry." She gets up carefully, feeling him slip out of her as she moves. She puts her skirt right as he tucks himself back into his pants.

"Don't be sorry," he tells me. "That was amazing."

"It really was," she agrees, looking around. They are alone. She doesn't think anyone stumbled outside during their interlude. If they had, they hadn't noticed. It is pretty dark behind the building. "So..." She lets the words drag out, not sure what to say.

"So," he echoes, smirking as he fixes his belt.

"So I don't do this kind of thing."

"Nor I," he says with a shrug, "but there are first times for everything."

She nods. "So what's the etiquette here? Do I just say thanks and head home? Am I supposed to buy you dinner?"

He glances at his watch. "It's a bit late for dinner, but breakfast in a few hours could be tempting." He cocks his head, contemplating, and then adds, "Tell me about this home of yours."

"It's not far away," she says, unable to stop herself, unable to deny the little thrill that starts building again at the way he is looking at her.

He looks around, then reaches for her hand. "I can walk you there, if you want. I'm very interested in hearing about the things you don't normally do."

She takes his hand and leads him away from the wall and onto the main street. "I don't think you want to hear about that," she says. "I think you have ulterior motives."

"I may just want to fuck you again," he says, raising her hand to his lips in a gallant gesture, "and take my time about it this time."

"Already?" she asks, surprised. He's not an old man, but definitely older than the teenage boys who can go again and again without pausing.

"I assure you that my refractory period is minimal," he says, and she feels a jolt of pleasure at the way he uses words. "I'm eager for another chance, if you'd have me." She stares at him, at that sensual mouth that is clearly attached to an intellectual brain, and her nipples harden.

"That sounds like a great idea," she tells him, biting her lip. "My place is just a few blocks away... and I probably have something you can eat for breakfast."

"Good," he says, "I have an early morning."

"Me too," she agrees. "But tonight still has many hours left."

$\mathcal{2}$

$\mathcal{S}$he opens the door to her place, frantically trying to recall just how messy she had left it when she went out a few hours ago. "Prepare yourself," she warns him. "I have a dog."

"I like dogs," he says and follows her inside to be greeted by Samwise, her black lab. Samwise is as happy as ever to see her again, and just as excited to meet her companion, and she wonders for a moment just how crazy she is to be bringing a complete stranger back to her home. But dogs are supposed to have a good sense of character. She watches her new friend kneel down to pet Samwise, sees how entranced her dog is with the newcomer, remembers that cock thrusting inside her, and decides she doesn't care about safety tonight. If she ends up on the news after being murdered, at least she will have had a few good orgasms first. "I'll have to take him out," she says. Her new friend stands up, reaches behind him to grab the leash from the hook on the wall, and clips it to Samwise's blue collar.

"Let's go," he says.

"Do you have a dog?" she asks, as they stroll slowly down the street.

He looks wistful, but shakes his head. "I did."

"Past tense?" she asks.

"Yeah…" He lets the word drag out, and she realizes that he is wondering how much to share, likely wondering how much she wants to know. She doesn't even know his name. She doesn't think she wants to know anything about him. She just wants the dog to go so that they could go inside and fuck again.

"Samwise is a great dog," she comments, saving him from sharing anything else. "He's good company."

"Does he mind company?" he asks, and she catches the undertone. Does she often bring strangers home?

She shrugs. "I don't think so." She looks over at him, heat streaking through her as she remembers those hands on her skin, those lips against hers. "I guess we will see how he feels about loud noises from the bedroom."

He smiles in a way that is all promise. "My dog used to sleep in the bed with me. Does he normally stay in there with you?"

She nods, pausing as Samwise finishes his business. "Yeah. But sometimes I boot him off the bed, especially if he's being a jerk and rolling all around. I don't think he'll go nuts if we kick him out tonight."

"Good," her new friend says as they head back to her house. She lets Samwise off the leash when they get inside, and he wanders off into the kitchen, losing interest in them and focusing on his food bowl.

"So," she says, staring at this sexy stranger next to her front door.

"So," he echoes, waiting for her.

"Is this the part where I offer you a drink?" she asks, floundering.

"Are you trying to get me drunk?" he comments, grinning.

"No," she answers, a grin growing on her face as the air heats up between them again. "But I have plenty of stuff to drink in the kitchen."

"Do you have ice?" he asks.

"Um... yeah," she tells him. "This isn't Greece. Why? You want a cold drink?"

He steps toward her, pushing her against the wall, hands on either side of her body as he leans in. "I had an idea of what I might do to you with some ice," he whispers. "You are so hot. I need to cool you down a little bit."

"And how would you do that?" she asks, voice low against his mouth.

He looks down the hall at the door to her bedroom, then in the other direction toward the kitchen. "Come with me." She follows him into the kitchen, and he lifts her onto the island across from the sink and the stove. She watches as he walks over to the refrigerator and presses the button on the front to get a handful of ice. Most of these he tosses casually into the sink, but he keeps one, holding it up to her as he approaches, fitting himself between her legs where she sits on the counter.

"Now," he says, trailing the piece of ice along the edge of her jaw to her mouth, a brief biting cold, and then he pulls it away, leaning back from her with an appraising glance. "Now I want to look at you," he tells her. "Take off your shirt."

She obeys, sliding the long-sleeved sweater over her head to reveal the plain white tank top beneath. She tosses the shirt behind her on the countertop. He nods, taking the ice and running it swiftly along her collarbone. She shivers, the melting water dripping down to wet the top of her tank top. Her nipples harden in anticipation. He leans in to kiss her, and she wraps herself around him, eager for more. He tugs the front of her tank top down to reveal one breast, taut nipple standing erect as he pushes down the edge of her bra. He teases her nipple with the ice, then, at her gasp, bends to replace the cold with the heat of his mouth. He sucks hard for a moment, his other hand reaching over to free her other breast, dexterous fingers caressing her naked skin. She wraps her hands around his head, pushing him to her. He pulls back, lips pursing to blow on her wet skin, sending shivers of delight across her body. "So lovely," he murmurs, then moves to suck the other nipple.

She moans, and then he stands up, slides the ice cube into his mouth, and lifts her tank top over her head. Her bra follows, sliding down her arms to be tossed casually to join the sweater behind her.

"Yes," he whispers, bending again to face her breasts, cold tongue licking and teasing as his hands press against her back. "Perfection," he says, one finger rubbing her nipple while his tongue licks the other. She leans into him, the cold against her nipples matching the heat between her legs. He looks up at her, a wicked grin, and then he kneels on the floor, his head even with the countertop, and slowly slides her skirt up over her thighs. "Now," he says, voice thick around the ice still in his mouth, "let me see what we have here." He pushes her back on the island so she leans on her elbows, looking down over the hills of her breasts to see his face between her thighs.

She marvels at the sight. *There is nothing sexier than a man looking up from between spread legs, eyes dark with intent, and mouth ready with promise.*

"Oh no," he whispers, fingers reaching out to touch her panties. "This will not do." He reaches up to find the edge of her panties and begins sliding them down her legs. "I will not have these in her way again. I want to have all of you."

As her panties slip off her legs and fall to the floor, he leans in again, fingers rubbing gently against her, a soft promise, and then his mouth, cold from the ice, but warm all the same closes over her. She hisses from the combination of hot and cold, pulling away from him unconsciously, and he grabs her hips and yanks her back toward him, his mouth meeting her with a long luscious lick from end to end. "Oh yes!" she moans, heels pressing into his shoulders.

"You like that?" he whispers against her skin, hot breath and cold tongue combining to make her squirm, his fingers rubbing up and down again her clit.

"Yes!" she tells him, pressing close against him.

"Tell me how you like it," he says, fingers sliding slowly up and down and then back and forth, to be replaced by his mouth in the same motion. He eases a finger inside her, pressing gently up, and she shudders against him, his tongue a slow steady rhythm against her clit.

"Like that!" she gasps, "Just like that!" She opens her eyes, looking down her body to see him looking at her, his glasses slightly askew on his nose, and he buries his mouth against her, his finger joined by another as he presses in and out in a maddening tempo. She tenses, body flooding with desire, and then he pushes her over the edge, and she comes shuddering against him. He pauses, but doesn't move away from her, his warm mouth still tight against her skin. After a moment, he flicks his tongue and she jerks upward, sensitive skin rebelling.

"I need—" she tries to remember words. "I need—"

That tongue moves against her again, and the whisper of breath, "You need more?"

"Too much!" she stammers. "Pause!"

He chuckles, breath still teasing her aroused skin, but he pulls away. "Pause," he agrees, getting to his feet and staring down at her as she dissolves into a puddle on her kitchen island. When she opens her eyes again, he is still watching her, a satisfied smile on his face. She manages to prop herself up on her elbows, willing life to come back into her legs, and grins at him.

"Yeah," she comments. "That was pretty awesome." She thinks of the ice in the sink, likely melted by now. "Definitely cooled me down."

"Now I suppose I'll have to get you all hot and bothered again," he muses. "I guess we should move to the bed."

3

*S*he leads him to her bedroom, fingers gently cradling his, body eager but willing to be patient. Happily, there aren't too many clothes strewn about the place. She had done most of her costume changes in the bathroom, so all of the rejects are hanging haphazardly from the towel bars in there. She makes a mental note to try to get to them before he goes in there, if he goes in there, then decides it doesn't matter. It isn't like she will see him again. She doesn't need to impress him with her tidy household. She doesn't need to cook for him, or learn his habits, or meet his parents.

All she is going to do is fuck him again… and maybe again before the night is over and she has to go back to reality. The months ahead loom in front of her, and she shakes her head.

Tomorrow. She will deal with everything tomorrow.

Tonight is just for her.

She looks up at him as they near the bed, then gives him a gentle push so he sits on the edge. He grins as she kneels on the floor before him, taking one of his feet in her hands.

"These should definitely come off this time," she tells him, tugging the shoe off and tossing it gently aside. "These too," she murmurs, pulling off the other shoe and both of his socks, revealing nice feet with long toes to match those glorious pianists' fingers. She wonders idly if he plays an instrument. She takes one of his hands, moving the finger to her mouth and sucking the tip, noting the trimmed nails. Maybe. His hands are delicate. She can taste herself ever so faintly on his skin, and she kisses his palm. His other hand slips behind her head, stroking her hair and running down her neck.

She turns her attention to his shirt, those damn buttons calling her name. She pops one near the top, reveling in the inch of skin it reveals. "I have wanted to do this," she tells him, punctuating each word by tugging on a button, "since I first laid eyes on you."

He watches her, eyes burning with desire. "Were you undressing me with those eyes?" he whispers, both hands straying down her body, one holding a breast while the other slides around her hip. He leans forward, kissing her neck. She pushes his shirt off of one shoulder, revealing a finely muscled chest, smooth pale skin that says he doesn't spend much time outdoors without a shirt on. In the dim light of the room, she can see the lines of muscles she hasn't guessed at beneath the simple clothing, but should have recognized from the easy way he held her against the wall.

He is strong, biceps toned and able, a runner's body, a swimmer's body, a body that she wants to have naked underneath her as soon as possible. She kisses his neck, running her hands under his shirt and up his back, then sliding the shirt all the way off his other arm. She strokes his skin, reveling in the knowledge that tonight, just for tonight, he is all hers.

Her hands find his belt while she kisses along the line of his neck and shoulder, her fingers undoing the buckle and tugging it free from his pants. The button is next, easily coming free before she slowly unzips him, hands slow and yet still so eager as she pushes his pants aside.

"Lay back," she tells him, and he obeys, that glorious chest stretched out against the dark sheets. She takes a moment to appreciate the image of this man in her bed, knowing it will sustain her for the next few months. She tugs his pants off quickly then, sliding them down to the floor and pushing them out of the way. His boxers are next, and then she is kneeling on the floor next to her bed, taking the length of him in her hands before leaning down to lick the tip ever so gently. He lets out the tiniest sound, hips straining for more, to get closer to her.

"Now, now," she murmurs against his skin, one hand slipping down to cup the soft skin of his balls, tongue circling the tip of that glorious cock again, moving away from him as he presses toward her, keeping him at the same distance. "Patience is a virtue."

"Virtue is overrated," he mumbles, hands snaking around to press against her head, trying to tug her closer. She keeps her mouth on the end of his cock, but uses both of her hands to press his hands to the bed next to his hips.

"Not tonight," she tells him. "Tonight you're all mine, and I'm going to take my time with you." She sucks him fully into her mouth then, a few quick hard strokes up and down, enough to elicit a gasp and a groan, and then goes back to teasing the head again. "Or I could speed things up, if you prefer," she offers.

His hand runs over her head and strokes the curve of her neck and shoulder. She looks up to see him looking down at her, no doubt enjoying the same view she had enjoyed in the kitchen. "I am at your complete disposal, madam," he says cordially.

4

The professor arrives at her office the following morning, refreshed, satisfied, and ready for the new semester to begin. She is actually early, having woken up tired, but content, body languid in that way only a night of great sex can accomplish. Her new friend had gone home in the early hours, leaving without a promise to call, without words, without anything expected or lingering, except the kiss he gave her right before he left. She hadn't learned his name. It had been perfect. Perfect enough to let her wake without begrudging the early hour, enjoy her coffee with a pep in her step, and even get to campus without cursing the rush hour traffic.

She walks inside with plenty of time to print out her syllabi and walk them over to the mail room for copying. She is ready for the semester to begin on Monday. Another year teaching at Abraxus Tasker College, one half of the tiny Literature department. The school does have an entire English department devoted to rhetoric and composition, but the literature offerings have always been small, only one required class for all majors, a tiny part of their four-year program. Sometimes, she wonders if it's enough, but then she is glad to have a job teaching at all, and devotes herself to making her one chance with the students matter. She does love teaching.

Sitting down in the auditorium, she misses Jim Spenser, her old companion in the literary trenches. He retired last year, and though she knows they hired his replacement over the summer, a Dr. Jack Spelling, she hasn't met him yet. She'd been away at a conference during the hiring process, though she'd read some of his articles and been impressed. Dr. Spelling has a way of making Shakespeare relevant, and she knows that is why Abraxus hired him. She idly wonders how old he is or what he looks like. None of his articles have an accompanying picture.

Since she knows they will be working closely together, she hopes they will get along the way she did with Jim, that the new-comer will agree with her approach and not get too caught up in the English department drama. It had been tempting when she first arrived five years ago to get overwhelmed, the cacophony of forty writing professors arguing over textbooks and assignments and the importance of grammar, but Jim had guided her away from that maelstrom, and the years have proven the wisdom of that counsel.

She holds a tenure track position in a related field, of course, but at Abraxus Tasker College, English Composition and Literature are separate departments. She and Jim could make their own decisions about textbooks and syllabi and procedures without needing to conform with the rest of the English department. Such academic freedom in higher education is a privilege, and she will fight to maintain it in the coming years, hopefully with Dr. Jack Spelling at her side. She sighs, looking around the auditorium and seeing acquaintances but no real friends. She is going to miss Jim this year, his company, his old man sense of humor, and his voice of reason whispering in her ear, especially during meetings.

She settles into her seat, lifting the small table from the side and flipping it over to form her desk, readying herself to sit through the day of meetings—the beginning of semester announcements, sharing of new policies, reiteration of old information—all the usual in-service information for the Friday before classes started.

It shouldn't be too bad, she tells herself. A little meet and greet for the new hires, a little chit chat with colleagues she hasn't seen over the summer break.

She feels someone watching her as she pulls out her tablet and looks around. Normally, she would sit with Jim during these meetings, the two of them whispering or passing sarcastic notes to pass the time, but now she is alone. She doesn't find the source of the gaze and shrugs it off.

Of course, someone is watching her. They'd all just gotten back from break. Everyone is scanning faces, identifying friends and exchanging pleasantries. She does her part, not really looking around for anyone, her thoughts occupied with the to-do list for the afternoon, a few minor things to complete before classes start on Monday. She turns on her tablet, racking her brain for the wifi password that she hasn't used in three months.

The morning passes in a blur of email and updates, and the lunch break is only minutes away. She thinks she might sneak away to her office for the afternoon, deciding she has enough professional development planned for the semester that she can skip the sessions today.

She is sort of listening to the conversations as everyone stands up, but still mostly in her own head when a familiar voice calls her back to reality. She knows that voice, has heard it pleading, commanding, whispering, and promising for hours last night. "I'm sure she will, ma'am," her lover says.

She looks up from her tablet, eyes widening in horror as her dean introduces the newest member of the department. "Meet Dr. Jack Spelling," Dean Hendrickson is saying, the small woman standing next to where the professor is still sitting in her seat. Her boss looks right at her, eyeing the tablet with disapproval, knowing she hasn't been paying attention. The professor quickly stows her tablet in her bag, getting awkwardly to her feet, trying not to look at a face that she has seen make all manner of expressions unexpected in a co-worker. Dean Hendrickson gestures at Dr. Jack Spelling.

"He's in Jim's old office," she continues. The dean looks back and forth from the professor to her lover. "This is Dr. Jacoby," she introduces her. "She's right next door to you. She can show you the ropes."

"I'm looking forward to it," Jack says, his voice a promise of pleasure to come. Dr. Jacoby tries to ignore the frisson of desire that spirals up from her core at the sound.

Office Hours

She puts her hand out awkwardly to shake his, and as his fingers touch hers, she remembers where those hands have been, and a tiny shiver rises from between her thighs. "Nice to meet you," she says quietly. Then she remembers herself, and adds, "Have you moved in yet? Are you needing the tour, or did you get your bearings already?"

That wicked smile teases the edges of his mouth, but his words are cordial enough. "I had the new faculty orientation yesterday, so I think I know where things are," he tells her. "Would you mind if I asked for guidance as things come up?"

"Not at all," she replies, turning back to the dean. One thing is certain—this is going to be an interesting semester.

5

Dr. Jacoby doesn't see Jack again until Monday evening after classes end. It has been a hectic day spent cycling through attendance rosters and syllabi while reassuring the new students that they are in the right place. She sinks into her office chair with a sigh, removing the friendly "Ask Me!" button that she wears for the first week and hanging it on the bookshelf behind her. She kicks off her shoes beneath the desk, glad to be rid of them. She never wears uncomfortable shoes, and certainly won't do it knowing she is going to spend the day on her feet, but it is always a pleasure to take off her boots, relishing the feel of her feet free beneath the desk. She glances out the open door of the office, and seeing no one in the visible hallway, listens carefully.

No one seems to be around. It is late, after all, the last classes of the day finished up about a half hour ago, students scampering to waiting cars and faculty drifting home to waiting bottles of wine.

She logs into her computer and turns on her music player, choosing something upbeat enough to motivate her to get through at least a little bit of work before she calls it a day. Since no one is around, she turns up the volume, and soon she is typing away, happily yell-singing the words along with the music.

She has no idea how long she has been in the zone when she hears a soft noise behind her, a polite cough. She freezes, word dying on her lips as she stops. She immediately turns down the volume and slowly spins to see who is standing in the doorway.

Please don't be the dean, her mind chants, *please don't be the dean.*

It isn't the dean.

It is Dr. Jack Spelling, standing in the doorway of her office like he belongs nowhere else, and she finds herself sitting up straighter, tucking her feet beneath her chair, wondering how long he has been standing there watching her one-woman concert.

"Dr. Spelling," she manages after an awkward silence while he continues to stare at her. "Was I disturbing you? I didn't think anyone was still here."

"Do you often put on concerts after everyone goes home?" he asks, and there is that sexy lilt in his voice, and suddenly she wants him to come into her office, slam the door, and have his way with her right on top of her desk. She closes her legs, willing the image away, the papers askew on the floor, pen cup rolling away as he raises her dress... She takes a deep breath and looks away from the desk back to where he stands.

She shrugs guiltily, "Maybe?" After a pause that threatens to turn into something else, she asks, "How was your first day?"

Jack shrugs, shoulders filling out that shirt in a way that makes her want to unbutton it all over again. "The usual," he says, "syllabus, learning names, you know the drill."

She nods. "I always suck at learning names. It takes me forever."

Jack chuckles, "I have to say you suck very well, Dr. Jacoby. And I have no doubt you prove an adept learner. As for names..." He trails off, body leaning slightly more into her office than before.

She leans back in her chair, then nods her head at the seat in front of her desk, inviting him to sit. He reads her signal, stepping inside and sitting down. "I didn't think I'd ever see you again," she says bluntly. "I didn't think I needed to learn your name."

"Do you want to know it now?" he asks, and the question is filled with meaning.

She considers. Does she? It is one thing to have mind-blowing sex with a complete stranger, knowing it isn't going to last. It is another to continue to have mind-blowing sex with a co-worker that she will have to see every day. That is something she has always avoided. Maybe he has as well.

"Do you want to know mine?" she counters. He knows her last name, but her first name isn't posted anywhere at the college. Only her first initial is there: C.

He leans back in the chair, one ankle coming up to rest on his knee, his hands going behind his head. She sees that his hair is mussed, the ends wild in a curly mass around his face, and she wants to run her fingers through it again, tugging it up even more than it already is. "This could be..." He pauses. "Complicated."

She nods, knowing that while there isn't a specific rule against dating co-workers, the college doesn't exactly encourage it. "It could."

"Or it could be..." he pauses again, this time a wicked smile crossing his face, "wonderful."

"Go on," she tells him, liking that grin, liking the thrill that fills her chest even more.

He puts his leg down and leans forward. "This could be exciting."

She glances behind him at the open door, hesitation draining out of her at the thought of fucking him again right there in her office. "It could," she repeats. He sees where she is looking and stands up, eyes watching her as he slowly slides the doorstop out of the way and lets the door shut firmly, leaning against it, hand cradling the handle behind his back. She stands up, walking to stand in front of him. He reaches for her instantly, long arms wrapping around her back and tugging her close for a kiss. He tastes like mint, and she pulls the gum he's been chewing into her mouth. They both stumble awkwardly backward, narrowly missing the chair to bang against her desk. He lifts her easily on to it, hands reaching down to push her dress up her thighs, fingers sliding her panties aside.

"Dr. Jacoby," he breathes into her open mouth, "you're so wet for me."

She begins unbuckling his belt, fingers clumsy in her haste, and is pleased to find him hard and ready for her. "Dr. Spelling," she tells him, stroking the length of him in both palms, "you're so hard for me."

He braces himself on the desk with one hand, the other still pressing against her flesh, and kisses her savagely, sucking her lip into his mouth and taking back the gum she'd taken from him.

"You want me?" he asks into her mouth. "You want me here, now, like this?"

"I want you," she tells him, hands pulling him close, then releasing him to grab his hips and press him between her legs. "I want you to fuck me right here on this desk."

He groans as he enters her, his hand holding her panties aside just long enough for him to slide inside, and then one hand is on her lower back, pressing her to him, and the other is on the back of her head, fingers twisting in her hair.

"Yes!" she moans into the kiss. "Fuck yes!" There is a small crash as the cup of pencils she keeps on the edge of her desk flies to the floor. She ignores it. He grabs her ass to lift her to a better angle, and then she hears nothing except their harsh breaths and the sounds of their bodies together, senses focusing on the feeling, losing herself in the pleasure as he brings her to the edge and crashing over it.

6

A week later, Dr. Jacoby is sitting in her office, shoes kicked off under the desk, brain exhausted. She hits send on the last email, and her hands fall to her lap, fingers absently rubbing along her thighs where the buckles of her garters rest. It has been a long day, but punctuated by secret thrills as a new sensation would rub against her bare flesh. She wears tights occasionally, so the material against her legs isn't foreign, but it has been a while since she wore stockings with garters. This morning, she made sure that her dress is long enough to cover everything—no need to flash students with things they have no business seeing. But now that classes are over for the day, she is lingering in her office, waiting to see if Dr. Spelling will be around. He has another class after her last one for the day, but he should be finishing up any minute now. She expects to hear his voice in the hallway soon, no doubt accompanied by a female student eager for some one-on-one time with her handsome professor. Dr. Jacoby isn't the only one to find Dr. Spelling attractive.

She waits for a little bit, just relaxing in her comfortable desk chair, letting her hands wander over her bare flesh, relishing in the naughtiness of touching herself in her office. The door is open, but no one can see her without walking inside, and she will hear them approach since she doesn't have any music on. There is little risk of discovery, but it is still fun to play at work. She thinks of hands on her skin, fingers sliding under her dress, followed by soft butterfly kisses and the warmth of breath, and then a hot tongue against—

She hears voices down the hall, and quickly removes her hand from beneath her dress. The sound continues for a few, quiet and comfortable, a deep rumble that she knows is Dr. Spelling, a higher voice that no doubt belongs to one of his students. All of the girls find reasons to visit him during his office hours. He is charming.

But tonight, he is hers.

She waits a little bit longer, catching a word here and there, knowing that their discussion of the assignment is long over, and the student is reaching for reasons to stay. Finally, Dr. Jacoby is tired of waiting, and she knows the feeling Jack must have right now, waiting for the student to leave him alone. She always appreciates it when a colleague rescues her from a clingy student. She can do the same for Jack now.

She slides on her shoes, sensible heels this time instead of her boots, and grabs her keys, letting her office door slide shut behind her. Her heels make a light tapping sound as she walks down the hall to Jack's office. She knows he can hear her coming.

"Let me know if you have any more questions, Bree," he says as she comes into view in his doorway. He looks at her, a slow smile crossing his face, his eyes sliding up her body as Bree turns around in the chair to see who has arrived. Dr. Jacoby flashes the student her best professorial look, friendly but done for the day. She turns back to Jack, whose face is all business again. "Ah, Dr. Jacoby," he says, addressing her over Bree's head. "I had a question for you." He smiles politely at his student, but the message is clear.

Bree stands slowly, angling her body to show her cleavage and lowcut shirt as she grabs her bag from the floor by her chair. "Thanks, Dr. Spelling," she breathes. "I really appreciate it."

"Any time," he replies, and then she is walking out of the door and down the hallway.

Dr. Jacoby waits a beat, lingering in the doorway until the footsteps fade away. "Any time?" she repeats. "You're so helpful, Dr. Spelling."

He turns back to the computer situated on the short side of his L-shaped desk, clicking the mouse a few times as he finishes up some work. "Always," he assures her.

"Am I disturbing you?" she asks, stepping into his office.

"No," he says, shaking his head. "I actually did have some questions for you," he adds, shuffling through some papers on his desk, his body sideways to where she stands across from his desk. She walks over to him, stepping around the desk to the right to stand behind his chair. He gives her a quick glance over his shoulder, smirks a little, and then returns to his papers.

"What's on your mind, Dr. Jacoby?" he asks in a perfectly even tone.

"I don't know," she murmurs, running a hand through his hair and leaning down to kiss the side of his neck. "I thought I'd come harass a colleague for a bit." She nibbles a little on his skin, earning a soft sigh as he relaxes into her. "Something to pass the time between grading."

"You aren't supposed to be grading," he says quietly, one hand reaching back to stroke the line of her ass through her skirt, the other still clicking the mouse here and there as he opens and closes windows on the computer. "Not yet, anyway. And aren't these your office hours? You're supposed to be here for your students." His hand pauses as he reaches her thigh, no doubt discovering the small bump of the garters, and he spins his chair to face her, computer screen forgotten.

"I'm always here for my students," she replies, reaching down to stroke him through his pants. "Like you, I'm a dedicated professional."

"I hope you didn't wear this for your students," he says, both hands sliding up her legs and lingering on the top of her stocking, fingers stroking the bare flesh of her inner thigh. "Definitely a professional, but not in this field."

"I can't be extra helpful for my students?" she asks, unzipping his pants and reaching inside to pull out his hard shaft.

He gasps as she touches him, hands moving from under the front of her dress around to squeeze her bare bottom. "Not like this, Dr. Jacoby," he growls. "You can only be extra helpful for me."

She sinks to her knees before him, forcing him to abandon her ass. His hands settle on her shoulders. "Giving me orders, I see," she says. "I don't know if you're in a position to be giving the orders quite yet. I'm the one with seniority in this department." She breathes on the tip of his cock, watching him harden even more before her. "You should listen to me. I have some valuable institutional knowledge that will help you fit in here."

"I will never dispute your seniority in this department," he swears, face eager as he watches her, "and I hope I continue to fit in here." His hand reaches down between their bodies to cup between her legs.

"I'm glad we sorted that out," she giggles, then glances to her left where the stack of papers still sat next to his keyboard, the pile level with where her head is. "Let me guess," she says, leaning down to lick the tip of his cock as he leans back in his chair again. "Trying to fill out your office hour form?"

He moans, glances at the open door, then over at the pile she is talking about. "How did you guess?"

"It's counter-intuitive," she says, letting the word stretch out against his skin as she licks the length of him. "You'd think engineers made it or something." He chuckles, and she asks, "Did you look at the sample they sent you?"

"Sample?" he groans, leaning back farther in the chair with his eyes closed, the back pressed up hard against the edge of the desk. If she pushes him back any more, the keyboard will jam into the monitor. His hand grips the long edge of the desk to his right.

She sucks him fast, deep and hard, twice, tugging him toward her, and then releases him, sitting back on her haunches to look him over, eyebrow raised. "Did you not read your email, Dr. Spelling? What kind of employee are you?"

He chuckles again, glancing at the door once more, then at the stack of papers to his right, the top few askew where his hand has bumped them, and finally down at where she kneels before him.

31

"The kind who teaches literature," he says, "and can't be bothered with little things like forms."

"You'd better start paying attention to little things," she admonishes, a hand reaching up to undo one of the buttons on her dress. "This is officially a STEM college, after all. They love their little details." She undoes another button, revealing the lacy top of her bra.

"Those," he says, "are not little details, Dr. Jacoby." She smiles and he bites his lip. She undoes another one. His hand reaches down to help with the next one, but she swats him away. His hand goes to his cock instead, giving himself a few quick pumps as he watches her unbutton the rest of the dress. "Lovely," he breathes, "down to the last detail."

"I am glad you approve," she says. "I want you to feel comfortable, of course."

"I'm feeling very relaxed right now," he answers.

She grins at him, then leans down to take that cock in her mouth again. "I am part of the welcome committee," she says against his skin.

"Does everyone get such a welcome?" he asks.

She looks up at him, his cock in her mouth, then slowly licks the tip. "Oh no," she says. "This is a special occasion."

"It definitely is," he breathes.

"Now," she says, reaching into his pants to cup his balls, "you are going to fill out that form."

"You can help me later."

"I am helping you now," she says, giving him a squeeze, "and you will do it now."

He smirks, then reaches for the stack of papers. He pulls out the yellow form in question, placing it on top of the pile. "And if I do?"

"Then I will see if you've done it properly, gotten all those details in the right place," she tells him, lazily swirling her tongue around him.

"And if I have?"

"Then I will have to have this cock in my pussy while I look it over," she promises, sucking him deep again, keeping her head below the level of the desk just in case someone walks by in the hallway. He groans, and she hears the shuffling of paper and pen as he fills out the form. She keeps up a delicious rhythm, enough to get him excited, but not enough for him to come. She wants way more action tonight before they are through. After a few moments, the pen hits the desktop, and she looks up at him.

"It's done," he says, face red with excitement, the flush disappearing into his collar. She reaches up and unbuttons his shirt, pushing it away from his chest, following that heat down his belly and along that delicious muscle right above his cock. She pulls his pants and boxers down, pushing him back onto the chair, then turning them both around to face the computer. She settles herself on his lap, his hands holding her ass, that hard cock pressing into her, sliding inside so easily, and she sinks into the feeling for a moment before remembering herself. His hands slip around her hips, reaching up to caress her breasts as she moves slowly up and down. He kisses her neck, squeezes her nipples, and she almost forgets why she is there.

"Dr. Jacoby," he whispers against her skin.

"Yes," she moans, moving up and down again, his cock pressing in all the right ways inside her.

"How did I do?"

"You're doing fine," she mumbles, picking up the rhythm as she splays her fingers flat on the desk in front of her, using it to push up and down faster.

"The form," he murmurs against her neck. "How is the form?"

She reaches around blindly to grab the yellow paper and scans the form briefly, seeing that he actually has filled it in properly—she's seen many people put the wrong information in the wrong spot—then she stops, stands up, turns around to face him, wraps her legs around him, and slides that cock back inside her, her breasts pressing against his bare chest.

He moves her faster, hands lifting her and tugging her to him for a passionate kiss. "Perfect form," she whispers against his lips as the slow burn spins up from her belly, "as always, Dr. Spelling."

7

"Don't forget to read all of the Dickinson poems for next time, plus the bio," Dr. Jacoby announces, glancing at the clock a final time. "And there's a quiz online. Please take it before you come to class next week," she adds, raising her voice slightly to be heard over the sudden shuffle of notebooks closing and zippers opening. The class empties slowly, students waiting on one another to continue conversations as they leave. She busies herself at the computer up front, gathering up her folders, shuffling papers into manageable piles, brain running through her after-class checklist.

She is fairly certain she covered everything she meant to. She collects the few sticky notes she had jotted concepts on, checking each one off the mental roster she has for the class—Poe, Virginia, "Annabel Lee," "the Raven," Baltimore, Election Day—when a soft shuffle catches her attention. She looks up, expecting to see a student with a question, and is rewarded with a handsome Dr. Spelling instead. He stands just inside the doorway, the last student having left and the door closing with a soft thump. He cocks his head and looks her over, a slow grin crossing his face.

"Dr. Jacoby," he says, "you look good enough to eat."

She blushes, leaning down and resuming her piling—graded assignments on the bottom, then notes from today, then the homework they just turned in, and then attendance sheet on top. She needs to keep things straight as she stacks them or she'll never figure out what assignment belonged where. "And are you hungry, Dr. Spelling?" she asks, straightening her pile and looking up to drink him in.

His shirt is dark today, the top button at the collar undone since he is probably done teaching for the day. It is still tucked into his pants, the dark leather of his belt visible. She catches the slight bulge of his crotch and lets her eyes wander slowly back up to his face, letting him watch her appreciation. His hair is a bit wild, like it always is by the end of the day, the effect of running his hands through it as he taught. She thinks it must make his students laugh, the dark curls nearly standing on end after hours of classes. She wants to run her hands through it now.

He walks down the aisle between the tables to the front of the room where she stands, leaning against the front row and tilting his head. "I'm always hungry for you," he whispers, the words making her shiver.

She glances at the door, the small glass rectangle showing the hallway beyond clearly. The lights are still on out there, meaning that someone is still moving around and triggering the motion-sensor lights, but she can't see anyone out there. The building will empty out at this time, but there can still be a few students wandering around, searching for professors' offices or for other students. They aren't nearly alone, not like when they meet in their offices. She looks at where he leans against the table, the two chairs on the far side, and a naughty idea begins to form. It is risky, though. Much riskier than anything else they've done.

He seems to follow her thoughts, eyes moving from her to the lectern that stands a few feet from him, up from the floor on a small elevated podium. She rarely uses it, preferring to move around and lead discussions, but every classroom has one.

"So, I've been encouraged to visit some classrooms," Dr. Spelling says conversationally, "to observe my colleagues and their teaching style."

"Is that right?" she asks, making a face. "Does the dean expect you to start lecturing like the rest of the tech people?"

He shrugs, those gorgeous shoulders lovely to behold as he moves. "Maybe?" He frowns. "Is that how we're supposed to do it here?"

She shakes her head. "No. Absolutely not. We're Literature people, Dr. Spelling. We generally have discussions and conversations about the reading. We aren't teaching someone how to code, or how to take an x-ray," she says, mentioning some of the other programs at the college. "We teach a general education course. Our job is to teach them how to think."

"Is that what general education is about?" he asks, raising one of the core questions in their discipline, a conversation she's had at many meetings, defending the arts to people who valued numbers and hard evidence. "Teaching them what to think?"

"Oh no," she replies, walking toward him, catching the shift in his question, the same trap many of the AS—Associate of Science—faculty would use, "not *what* to think—*how* to think." She shrugs. "We teach critical thinking skills, and that takes practice, and practice for us means discussion." She reaches out to take his hand, loving the heat that moves through her as their skin meets. She gives him a serious look. "Don't feel like you have to lecture here because that's how most of the classes are."

He brings her hand up to his lips, kissing it. "How do the students respond?" he asks. "Do they expect lectures?"

She nods, watching his mouth. "Sure! But they tend to open up once we start discussing the reading. You'd be surprised how much they get into it, even the poetry, once you let them know it's okay to relax and talk about it." She pauses, reading the face of a concerned colleague questioning his craft. "Why? Did they give you grief about something?"

"No," he says, tilting his head to the side, "not really. But they were definitely surprised."

"Why?" she asks, hopping onto the table to sit next to him.

He shrugs. "I recited some Shakespeare for them, and they were shocked that I had it memorized."

She nods, letting their still clasped hands fall to his thigh. "No doubt. Did they ask why you bothered?"

He laughs, "Not in so many words, but yes."

"They don't tend to value knowledge that isn't clearly practical here, not at first. That's what I spend most of my time teaching them—that it's okay to learn about something for its own sake—that knowledge doesn't have to have an immediate, practical use," she explains. She looks at him. "What poem did you recite?"

"The usual," he says, "'Shall I compare thee.'"

"I like that one." She squints at him, mouth curling up playfully as she slides her hand up his thigh. "Did you tell them it's about a guy? They tend to get thrown when I mention that."

He chuckles, his hand drifting to her thigh and stroking the outside. "No. I don't want to cause waves during my first few weeks here by explaining pederasty." He pauses, hand resting firmly against her, separated by the material of her skirt. "I focused on the words. I think they enjoyed the 'fair from fair' bit once I explained it."

"I love that part," she agrees, "and who wouldn't want to always remain lovely and desirable throughout time?" He winks at her, hands giving her a quick squeeze, and she stumbles back into work mode. "Do you usually read it from the book or do you recite it from memory?" she asks.

"Memory," he shrugs again, hand retreating back to touch the outside of her thigh. "I have a lot of Shakespeare in my brain."

"Occupational hazard," she admits. "I did Poe today, and I've done it so many times that I can recite 'The Raven' without looking down at the page." She looks at him, trying to rekindle the mood and knowing just how to do it. "How did you recite it?"

He looks at her, confused. "What do you mean?"

"Like, did you stand up front and bust out with it, or did you set it up on the overhead, or did you walk around and say it...?"

"I just stood up front and said it."

She smirks, letting her hand wander again. "I bet the girls loved that."

He laughs, leaning back a little to give her better access. "What? Why?"

She gives him a look, hand pressing against his cock through his pants. "It's a love poem, recited by a sexy professor. I bet most of the girls are drooling over you by the end of class."

"But will you be drooling over me, Dr. Jacoby?"

"I don't know," she says teasingly. "I'd have to hear it first."

"Seriously?"

She nods, removing her hand and leaning back on her elbows on the table, her skirt riding up to reveal more of her stockings than she ever shows in class. "Oh yes," she says dramatically, "Recite some Shakespeare for me, Dr. Spelling."

He smiles, and she can see him relishing the words as he speaks. "Shall I compare thee to a summer's day?" he begins, gesturing at her. "Thou art more lovely and more temperate…"

She sits up and clasps her hands at her chest, wowed by him even as he speaks the words she knows so well. She has always been a sucker for poetry, even back in high school. She may have specialized in American Literature, but she never lost her love of the Bard.

He glances behind them at the doorway, and seeing nothing, leans down, words decreasing to a whisper as he speaks against her lips, "and every fair from fair sometimes declines," he says, and then he is kissing her, and she runs her fingers through his hair. The kiss breaks after a moment, and he continues, hands moving down her sides and under the seam between her shirt and skirt to touch the bare skin of her midriff. "But thy eternal summer shall not fade," he murmurs against her chin, one hand reaching up to tilt her neck to the side and brush her hair aside so he can kiss the skin there, "nor lose possession of that fair thou ows't…" He finishes the words, leaving her breathless with lust and aching with desire.

"That was…" she begins, trying to find words between the pulsing rush of desire in her skin, "that was lovely." She takes a moment, breathing heavily, stirred by the depth of her response to him. "I hope you didn't deliver it in class like that," she says finally. She wants him to take her right there on the table, but he steps away from her, looks from her to the lectern and back again, face calculating.

"Oh no," he assures her, stepping up onto the podium. "I stood up here and said it."

She smiles and shakes her head. "I never stand up there."

He hops down and takes a few steps toward her. "Why not?"

She shrugs, letting him tug her off the table to her feet. "I don't know. I'm not a lecturer like that. It just doesn't seem to work."

"What doesn't work?" he asks. "Let me see you up there."

She obliges, humoring him, stepping up and behind the lectern, leaning her hands against the slanted top, gazing out at the classroom. "I'm supposed to stand here," she tells him, "and talk." She turns around to gesture at the white board behind her. "Though I don't know why anyone would. I can't even reach the board from here. I couldn't write anything down."

He approaches, stepping up behind her and wrapping his arms around her middle. She leans back into his embrace, letting herself relish the feel of him, the smell of him, his heat so close through his clothes. She molds her body to his, pressing back and feeling the stirrings of delicious hardness behind her.

"But Dr. Jacoby," he whispers in her ear, and she shivers, "others use PowerPoint presentations to teach. They don't write on the board."

She rolls her eyes. "They also use the same presentation from ten years ago," she mutters. "They can recite it in their sleep at this point."

He nods, sliding around to face her, wedging himself between her and the lectern. She glances at the door, seeing shapes moving by in the hallway, but no one opens the door and comes inside. She looks up at him, his face only a few inches above her own. "Can you recite it?" he whispers.

"Recite what?"

"Your lesson," he says, leaning down to trail small kisses down her neck and across her shoulder, tugging her sweater down as he does so. "You covered Poe today."

"You want to hear my lesson on Poe?" she asks, a bit breathless.

"I want to hear your recite some Poe," he says, hands reaching down to her thighs and sliding up under her skirt. He lingers on the stockings she nearly always wears now, then lets his hands slip up farther, stroking her clit with a forcefulness that makes her gasp, "under duress."

Her knees grew weak as he continued to press against her, heat and wetness building in her lower belly. "What kind of duress?" she squeaks, as he gives her a wicked grin, turns around to glance at the door, turns back to her, winks, and kneels before her, body hidden from view by the lectern. His hands slide around to cup her ass, and then he is lifting her skirt and ducking underneath it, his mouth meeting her clit with a long, succulent kiss. Her legs jolt and she nearly falls against him, hands pressing hard into his shoulders. "Oh god!" she moans, pleasure streaking through her.

"That's not the first line." His voice drifts up, his breath hot on her skin, his fingers sliding up her inner thighs to press against the edges of her opening.

"Please," she begs, wanting him to lick her again.

"That's not the first line, either," he replies, and he kisses the top of her thigh instead. "Focus, Dr. Jacoby."

"Once..." she says, letting the word trail off as he kisses her clit again, warm sparks shooting up into her lower belly. But then his mouth is gone. Waiting.

She ransacks her brain for the lines of poetry she knows by heart. She can do this. She deserves this. She knows this poem inside and out. She can totally do this.

"Once upon a midnight dreary," she begins, words sure and strong. She is rewarded by another long, wet kiss, followed by a strong finger slipping inside her.

"Yes..." he moans against her, encouraging, and she shudders.

"While I pondered," she continues, "weak and weary," and there is another of those licks, this time keeping rhythm with her words. "Over many a quaint and curious volume of forgotten lore," she says quickly, the words tripping over one another in her haste to get them out, and she is rewarded by solid sucking and another finger joining the first. She presses down on his shoulders, needing him to continue. "While I nodded," she says, and then he is nodding against her, his chin pressing into her lips and his tongue working magic against her clit, and those fingers rubbing in and out, in and out, "nearly napping," she breathes, and then there is a third finger, and she is nearly riding his hand now, one hand death gripping his shoulder and the other pressing him against her through the fabric of her skirt. "Suddenly, there came a tapping," she wheezes, and his fingers began a maddening rhythm that make her legs begin to shake, "as of someone gently rapping," she breathes, "rapping at my chamber door," she manages, and closes her eyes, sinking into the feeling, pressing herself into him. She is almost there when he pauses, breath hot against her as he says, "That's not the entire poem, Dr. Jacoby."

The fingers abandon her, leaving her feeling hollow and aching, and he pauses, face an inch away from where she wants him. She slides her skirt up around her belly, looking down at him, seeing his face where he kneels before her, his hair a wild mass of curls in every direction. She grabs a handful and presses him back against her, but he grabs the back of her skirt and tugs, pulling her away from him.

"Oh no, Dr. Jacoby," he says, "you'll have to do better than that."

She rallies, her brain trying to conjure the words while the aching builds. "Umm.." she says, stalling for time, "umm…" His hands slide up the back of her thighs, cupping her ass, thrilling but not the thrill she wants at the moment. "Tis some visitor!" she nearly shouts, the words coming to her in a rush. She is rewarded with another of those long kisses, his tongue licking long, his lips sucking hard. "Some late visitor entreating entrance at my chamber door," she continues in a rush, but at the word "door," she realizes that she has had her eyes closed again. She glances quickly at the door, seeing shapes in the hallway, but none near the glass. She hopes no one had walked by and peered in. She glances down at Jack's head buried in her crotch and pleasure jolts through her again, the thought of being caught at any moment an unexpected thrill along with the challenge of reciting poetry. "Only this," she finishes quickly, focusing on the building warmth and rising wave, "and nothing more!" At the final word, he slips three fingers inside her again, the rhythm enough to make her come almost immediately.

She shudders against him, breathing hard, seeing stars, and then sags against the lectern, leaning over him.

He chuckles, his breath warm against sensitive skin, and she jerks away, needing a moment. His hands retreat a safe distance to cup her ass again, and he chuckles again. "I need to see that ass," he orders, getting to his feet and spinning so the lectern was behind them. He lifts her easily, placing her on the edge of the lectern, her clit and vagina easily accessible. She tries to glance behind her at the door, but his hand is stroking her again, and she closes her eyes instead. "Yes..." she moans, and then he is pulling her slightly closer, throwing her legs over his shoulders and leaning forward.

"I want to see you squirm, Dr. Jacoby," he says, sliding closer to her, tugging her closer for another long kiss and suck of her clit and lips, "and I want to feel all of you," he says, and then his hands are under her, fingers sliding inside her with a sweet jolt, and his other hand lifting her even more into the air. She squeezes against his fingers, loving the feeling, and he leans forward for another long sucking kiss that has her shuddering against him. His fingers begin to move and she loses herself, coming hard again. "Oh, yes," he chuckles, moving one leg down from his shoulder to his waist, where it hangs limply, but leaving the other on his shoulder, looking intently at her.

"Hmm?" she asks dreamily.

"All this talk of chamber doors," he murmurs, "and here I thought we'd never get there." At this, his fingers begin slowly moving toward her ass. "Are you into other doors, Dr. Jacoby?" he whispers, leaning forward to give her another quick lick as his fingers explore deeper inside her.

"I don't know if Edgar Allan Poe would approve," she murmurs, "but I'm with Shakespeare on this one. I'm open to all doors." His finger slips inside her then, slow and careful, using the wetness of his mouth and her excitement to lube the way. She sighs, leaning down into his hand, and then he is licking her again, bringing her to the edge with sudden efficiency, and when she comes, he slips two fingers inside and she shudders against him.

"Again?" he whispers against her sensitive skin, but her legs are throbbing with fatigue and she needs to move. She shakes her head, bringing her legs down to the floor and sliding off the lectern. "I need you inside me," she says, all thought of discovery lost in her lust.

"Inside you where?" he asks, spinning her so he stands behind her. He steps off the podium, the few inches putting her ass at the perfect height for him. He undoes his belt quickly, positioning himself behind her, his hard length pressing against her opening. She is soaking wet from his mouth and her own excitement, so she doesn't think she will even need lube. He pulls her hard against his chest, kissing her neck, hands caressing her breasts under her shirt, reaching into her bra to squeeze her taut nipples. "Where do you want me inside you, Dr. Jacoby?" he whispers.

She glances at the door, noting that the hallway lights have gone out. No one has walked by in at least five minutes. The lights will turn on again if anyone does, their movement tripping the motion sensor in the hallway, though she wonders if either of them would even notice. She decides that she doesn't even care. "I want you to fuck me in the ass," she says, turning her head to see his face, her eager mouth claiming his lips, tasting him as he drives his tongue into her mouth.

"I thought you'd never ask," he says against her mouth, and then he is rubbing himself with her slickness, pressing the head of his cock against her opening, and he slides ever so slowly inside. She leans back hard against him, using gravity to help her slide onto him, his cock filling her in new ways. She reached the bottom of his cock, and then he lifts her ever so gently, letting her slide back down again. She moans and moves again, getting a rhythm going. She uses the height difference to her advantage, putting her full weight on her legs and feet as she moves on him, and his hands slip from cradling her ass to rub her clit again, his thumb sliding against her in the perfect pressure, and soon she is shuddering against him, the feeling of fullness echoing through her entire body.

"What do you think of the lectern now, Dr. Jacoby?" he asks, moving inside her, letting the moment build again.

"Quite delightful, Dr. Spelling," she breathes, sliding down his cock again. "You make me rethink my position on lecturing."

"I hope to discover all manner of positions with you," he replies, moving faster now, pushing up as she presses back. "Though this is definitely one of my favorites."

"It was the poetry," she admits, bracing herself against the lectern and moving even faster now. "I can't resist a good performance."

He presses himself deep inside her again, his thumb beginning that slow sweet stroking against her clit. "Is it good?" he asks, breathing hard as his own climax draws near.

"So fucking good," she answers, leaning back and finding his mouth with hers. "I find your performative skills to be quite enthralling!" And then she is coming hard and so is he, and they forget about words for a time.

8

$\mathcal{D}$r. Jacoby shifts in her desk chair, trying to figure out how to get the student sitting across from her to take the hint and leave her alone. Not that she minds talking to students, she doesn't at all, but he's been in her office for forty minutes already, she has emails piling up and forms to turn in before she heads home tonight, and she needs to catch the dean before she leaves for the day to sign off on her travel paperwork.

"Of course," she nods, "that's another one of the great things about Dickinson's poetry." Her end of the conversation has been reduced to agreement in the last few minutes, but he doesn't seem to get the hint. She turns her body away from him a little bit more so she's nearly facing the computer to her left, obviously clicking on an email and scanning it. "We can always get more from it each time we read it," she finishes absently, mouse clicking as she scrolls down the message.

William still sits in the chair across from her, leaning forward, face eager to continue the discussion. He is a good kid, she knows that, good looking too, but she doesn't have time for this kind of drawn-out discussion today. *Now, if I didn't spend so much time fucking my colleague…* Her mind observes sarcastically, but she shuts it down, skimming another email and deleting it.

"But what about—?" He begins anew, and she has to shut this down.

"I'm so sorry, William," she says bluntly, since he isn't catching any of her subtle hints to leave. "I have a ton of work to finish, and I have to turn this in before I leave today," she gestures at the computer screen, where her travel paperwork has finally opened, taking up most of the monitor. "I'd love to continue this chat, but another time."

"Oh, yeah!" he says, embarrassed and flustered as he starts gathering his bag. "Of course," he agrees, getting to his feet awkwardly. "Sorry to bother you."

"You're not bothering me," she reassures him, "not usually! I just have to get this done now." She smiles at him, then realizes she can see the small bulge of a semi-erection as he stands, and she looks quickly away, trying to forget the image. She tries never to think of her students that way.

Once, she had a terribly wicked dream about a current student and she had never been able to look him in the eye again. It was unfortunate because he was a great student, and she would have enjoyed more conversations with him, but she couldn't get the dream out of her head. Every time she saw him, her cheeks flamed with the memory. Why couldn't she be like some of the other faculty members who were perfectly willing to have sex with students? She can understand hooking up with a former student after the class is over—people meet lovers in all sorts of situations—but there are a few of her colleagues who are not so moral. She definitely has a problem with that.

She looks at William, knowing she could never bring herself to sleep with him, cute smile or not, sees the bulge again, and then she tries not to think of what William's cock would look like at full mast, how it would feel in her mouth. She nods at him, smiling brightly, feeling heat creep up her chest, "Have a good one, William," she says. "I'll see you next time."

"Sure!" he agrees. "Good luck with your paperwork."

And then he is gone, and the hallway is silent, and she is hard at work again. After a frantic thirty minutes, she thinks she might be finished. After another eight minutes, she has scanned the document for the last time. She has just pressed the print button when movement in her doorway has her glancing in that direction.

"Dr. Spelling," she smiles, always glad to see him. "How nice of you to drop by."

He smiles back, looking at the sea of sticky notes across her desk, "Am I disturbing you? I can come back another time."

She shakes her head, starting to gather them up, balling up the completed tasks with relish and tossing them into the recycling bin. "Actually, no. I just finished." She glances at the clock on the wall. "And I have exactly twenty-one minutes to get this to the dean's office for her signature."

"Nicely done," he congratulates. "Twenty-one minutes. That's not a lot of time."

"Isn't it, though?" she asks, her eyes inviting, and she gestures for him to come inside. "Shall we see how much we can accomplish in a few minutes?" He nods, moving to sit in the student chair, but she shakes her head, a wicked thought forming. "No," she tells him, "come here." She slides the rest of the papers from the small desk in front of her to her left so they sit on the computer desk instead, then picks up the cup of pencils, gives him a meaningful look, and places it on the bookshelf behind her. She's been finding random pencils on the floor for weeks now.

She adjusts her chair, letting her weight push it to the lowest setting so she is much closer to the floor, and gestures at the empty desk in front of her. "Sit."

He obeys, stepping around the desk to sit on top of it, his knees spreading so she can scoot her chair between them. "What's this?" he asks, glancing at the travel paperwork on top of the pile she just moved. "Going somewhere?"

"The International Shakespeare Conference," she tells him, hands reaching forward to touch him, wrapping around his back and tugging him forward a few inches. "I wanted to talk to you about it." She moves her hands down, unbuckling his belt as she speaks.

"Oh?" he asks. "I like talking to you." He moves his hands to rest on the table next to his hips, bracing himself as she opens his pants. "I also like when you do things like this." He closes his eyes for a moment, then rallies, returning to the conversation, "Your proposal?"

"They accepted it," she tells him, moving on to his button and zipper. "It's not until the summer, but I wanted to get the funding sorted out now before it's all gone."

She has his pants open, and she reaches in to pull out his cock, pleased as always to see how hard he already is for her. "Are you going this year?" she asks, then leans forward to take him into her mouth, relishing the hardness, loving how much joy this cock brings her. She leans back, releasing him, "I know you submitted a proposal."

He looks down at her, excitement at such a warm welcome on his face, "I am going," he says, then gasps as she draws him deep inside her mouth.

She releases him with a long pop. "Congratulations," she tells him, smile spreading on her face. "So we'll both be there ... together."

The word hangs between them, and she leans down to suck him again, but he puts a hand under her chin, lifting her face to look at her.

"Do you want to go ... together?" he asks, face hopeful.

"Do you?" she asks instead, not wanting to misunderstand his intentions. They have been fucking regularly for months now, but they haven't discussed a relationship, or the future, or anything like that.

Before he can answer, there is a noise in the hallway, a step, and then he is sliding off her desk, hands frantically trying to put his cock back inside his pants. There isn't enough time for him to fasten his pants before the visitor walks by, or even worse, walks in, so he dives under her desk instead, landing with a thump that Dr. Jacoby covers by loudly moving her chair back and then forward again. She scoots under the desk, the sides of the chair just clearing the desk surface as the person enters her office. Dr. Jacoby turns to take a drink from her water bottle, the drink giving her a moment to gather herself before she has to speak.

"Hello, Dr. Jacoby," the dean says, taking a seat across from her. "I hoped to find you still here."

Dr. Jacoby schools her face, trying not to think about the man hiding beneath the desk in front of her. "Dean Hendrickson," she begins, "I was going to come see you in a few minutes, actually."

"Call me Mary," the dean says, "No need to be formal."

"Okay Mary," Dr. Jacoby repeats, then hastily adds, "call me Celia." They share a smile, and then Celia turns slightly to scan her desk for the travel paperwork she casually tossed aside a few moments before, careful not to move her chair in case she hits Jack. She finds it, picks it up, and slides it across the desk to where the dean sits. "I have my travel packet for the Shakespeare conference this summer. I thought I would get it turned in sooner rather than later."

Celia leans forward, letting her legs and feet slip slowly down from where they have been curled up on the chair. She feels hands gentle against her feet, then they rest on both ankles, reassuring.

The dean leans forward and picks up the papers, eyes scanning them quickly. Celia uses the moment of distraction to put a hand on her lap, and a second later, Jack's warm hand is on top of it, solid and comforting. She feels her pounding heart beginning to slow, and she focuses on her boss. She knows that she and Jack have been flirting with discovery for months now, but nothing has been quite so close as this one. She tries to ignore the frisson of desire that rushes through her at the thought of the situation, Jack trapped under her desk with the dean feet away, only hidden by the wood of her desk, but she can't. Jack's hand slowly abandons hers and she brings it back up to the top of the desk. There is a moment when she can't feel him at all, and then a hand touches her calf, warm and familiar.

The dean is nodding in approval, "Yes," she says, scans something on the third page, then flips back to the top sheet. "Very nice. Perfectly done as usual." She looks up at Celia. "I can sign these here and then you can just interoffice them over to Millie at District."

"Great!" Celia agrees, then scans her desk for a pen. The cup of pencils behind her is the first thing she thinks of, so she spins the chair to retrieve them, thumping Jack in the process. There is a sharp intake of breath, which she covers with a sudden cough, hoping the dean hasn't noticed. She turns back more slowly, mindful of the man under her desk, and slides the cup across the desk to the dean. She is glad to see that a pen has found its way into the cup amid the random pencils.

The dean glances behind and around Celia's seat to the bookshelf, then at the cup. "That's an interesting place to keep your pencils," she observes, plucking the pen and beginning to sign.

"I keep knocking them over," Celia says without thinking, and then feels the blush work its way up her neck.

The dean pauses between signature and date, face curious as she takes in the simple desk, the reasonably sized office. "Are you typically rough on your desk?"

A snort works its way out before she can stop it, but she turns it into a self-deprecating chuckle. "I'm clumsy," she admits. "I'm always knocking things over with my bag when I leave." The dean nods, then turns her attention back to the papers. Celia stiffens suddenly, a quick breath turning into a soft cough, as a finger, soft and tentative, slides up from her calf and slips up to touch the bare skin of her inner thigh.

"That I can understand," the dean says, finishing her writing, and sliding the papers back over to Celia. "By the time I leave for the day, I'm too exhausted to see anything on my desk."

"I hear you," Celia says, nodding, trying not to let her face show that anything untoward is happening beneath the desk. The finger has been joined by others, and Jack's hand is slowly creeping up to stroke the tender flesh at the center of her thighs. She twists in the chair, moving her legs together, catching his hand between her thighs. "Some evenings I'm too tired to think about anything. It's like my brain reaches max capacity and shuts down."

The dean is nodding, still sitting, clearly not ready to leave yet. "And no wonder," she says, "with such a brain. Congratulations on being accepted for the conference. You may be a small department, but you're doing great things. We're grateful to have you!"

"Thanks!" Celia says, honestly touched by the praise, and trying not to think about the other places where she is being touched. The fingers have begun a slow slide back and forth within the trap of her thighs, tips grazing sensitive skin with each pass. "I'm grateful to be here!"

The dean leans forward, and Celia knows that whatever she is about to say is the real reason for her visit. "And Dr. Spelling?" she asks. "How is he settling in here?"

"Perfectly!" she replies, relaxing a bit as the hand stops moving, no doubt surprised to hear his name enter the conversation. "He's a great colleague."

"And I understand that he will also be attending the Shakespeare conference this summer," the dean says, clearly leading up to something. Celia adjusts again in the seat, and both of Jack's hands end up on the outside of her thighs, pressing against her skin.

Celia nods.

The dean gives her a look. "You know?" She raises an eyebrow. "Did he tell you today? He just told me earlier."

Celia nods again, brain trying to work out the timeline, "Yes, a few minutes before you got here. He was heading out for the evening."

"Are you two often chatting at the end of the day?"

Celia tries not to read into the question, knows that the dean is just asking the normal questions for a new faculty member, but she can't ignore the hands on her skin, the warm breath that has joined them, hot against her knees. She nods at the dean. "Sure! He's pretty great. And I know the students love him."

"Good," the dean says, "great to hear." She pauses, then takes a breath, clearly deciding to just say something. "I was thinking ... since both of you are going to the same conference."

Celia cocks her head, waiting for the question though she is pretty sure where this is going. The travel budget for the school is small. Larger departments often share accommodations during travel, men and women bunking together. Celia knows that she can say no, since she would be sharing with a man, and that's why the dean has come to ask her first, to see if maybe they can half the cost of the hotel room for the week. But she waits, letting the dean ask it. The breath on her knees has moved closer, and she opens her legs a little, letting the hands slip to stroke her inner thighs again.

"Would you be willing be share a hotel room with Dr. Spelling for the trip? Have you two gotten that friendly?" The dean gives her a serious look. "No pressure, Celia. You can say no. It's absolutely fine. But I thought that you two might have grown ... closer ... so I thought I'd ask."

Celia wonders just how much the dean knows and decides not to ask. The fingers move farther up her legs, and she squirms just a little, wanting him to continue the torture but also wanting to focus on the conversation.

She pauses, appearing to consider the offer for a long moment. Does she want to share a room with Jack Spelling? Absolutely. But does he want to share a room with her? They haven't discussed such possibilities, though the eager hands on her skin suggest that he may be in favor. Eventually, she nods, "That would be fine with me. I like Jack. We get along really well. It's fine with me as long as it's fine with him."

Celia is rewarded by hot breath against her inner thighs and two fingers slide against the center of her.

"Great," the dean says. "Excellent. I'm glad everything is working out up here."

"Definitely," Celia breathes as the fingers begin a slow slide in and out of her.

"I'm glad we had this chat," the dean tells her, then stands up. Celia slides forward a few inches in her chair, and the fingers move away to give her space.

"Me too," Celia agrees, then reaches for the paperwork. "I'll get this over to Millie right away."

"Perfect. I'll talk with Dr. Spelling about this tomorrow and we can get everything settled for the conference." The dean takes a look around the office, smiles at Celia, and turns to go. "Enjoy the rest of your evening," she says.

Celia is ready to reply, but then a warm tongue licks her, and any parting words she has in mind disappear. She makes a dismissive agreeable sound instead, and then the dean is leaving, the sound of her feet echoing down the hallway. The tongue continues its motion, and Celia sits in her chair, legs frozen between terror and pleasure, sinking further into desire. After a moment, there are no more footsteps, and they are alone. Celia slides her chair back, and Jack comes with her, lifting her skirt, face staring up at her from where he still sits on the floor.

"We get along very well, do we," he begins, then adds, "Celia?" She smirks, knowing that she has never actually told him her first name. The placard on her office door just has her first initial: Dr. C Jacoby. "Why didn't you tell me?" he whispers against her skin.

She squirms against him, heart filling with more than just liquid desire. "Come on," she says, "you know why. I can only imagine what you're thinking, you Shakespeare scholar." He grins, then leans in to lick her again. "Celia is supposed to be the ungettable get," she tells him, "the perfect unattainable goddess." She pauses as he kisses her again, waves of pleasure echoing through her, "the bitch who sends back flowers," she adds with a smirk, referring to the famous poem about Celia and her refusal to accept the speaker's advances, and he chuckles, the sound vibrating against her in delightful ripples.

"I'm not disputing the goddess part," he says, words poised between luscious licks, "and I would love to send you flowers, and be thrilled if you accepted them, though I will also understand if you send them back, smelling only of you," he says, referring to the rest of the famous poem. He stops, then gets up on his knees to give her a real look, dragging the chair closer so his face is level with hers. "And I'm so honored to have 'gotten' you," he adds, leaning close to give her a slow sensual kiss. She can taste herself on his lips, and she presses close, relishing the feel of him touching her, her hands winding in his hair.

"Take me then," she tells him, sliding forward in the chair, and reaching to pull him free of his pants again. He looks over his shoulder at the door, listens for a second, then turns back to her with a wicked grin, tugging the chair close by grabbing the arm rests and sheaths himself in a swift motion. Celia moans, biting her lip. He slides the chair back a few inches, then pulls her back to him, using the wheels to his advantage, setting a rhythm that has her writhing against him, legs hooked around his hips and urging him on. "Come for me!" he demands, "Come on my cock!" and then she is shuddering against him, legs locking to hold him close as their bodies shudder in unison. They hover for a long moment, their shaking breaths the only sound, and then he slides her away slowly, slipping out of her and sagging to sit on the floor in front of her. His hands drop from the armrests to her hips, and he rests his face against her thigh.

"Amazing," he breathes. "My Celia."

"Your Celia," she agrees, and he gets slowly to his knees again, folding her into a long, passionate kiss.

"Are we doing this then?" she asks when the kiss breaks and they are looking at one another openly, honestly. "Really doing this?"

He nods, face eager. "It's only been a few months, but I want more of this. I want more of you." He looks around the office. "And I want you in other places."

She cocks her head at him, confused. "Like the floor?" she asks, and he laughs.

"No!" He considers, then says, "Well, actually, yes, the floor would be lovely, but I mean that I want to see you outside of this place, outside of work, in public."

"You mean like a date?"

He nods. "Yes. I want to go out with you, spend even more time talking with you, and then bring you home and fuck you silly."

Celia smiles. "Sounds like a date to me."

"And I can't wait to go to the conference with you this summer. Together."

"And you're okay with mixing business and pleasure?" she asks, hope burning in her chest.

He kisses her again, long and slow, and the floor starts to look more and more promising. "Spending time with you is always a pleasure, whether it's business or not," he says. "I want you."

Office Hours

"And I want you," Celia breathes, fingers gripping him tightly. "But are you sure you will still want me this summer?"

He smiles at her. "My dear Celia, I already told you: you will never lose your fair for me."

Celia smirks, "Shakespeare again. He always knew how to get the girls into bed."

Jack raises an eyebrow. "A bed, you say? How about we go to my place tonight and check out my bed?"

"Again so soon?" she teases. "You do have a remarkable refractory period, Dr. Spelling."

"Call me Jack," he tells her. "Tonight, in my bed, call me Jack."

She knows what he is really saying and what goes with it. She thinks about the consequences, the future, the possibilities, and decides to take the wild leap.

"Do you have ice, Jack?" she asks, smirking, ready to face the world beyond her office hours.

AbraXus Tasker College
Sophmore Year

Tutoring CENTER

Ali Whippe

DEDICATION

For all the quiet ones

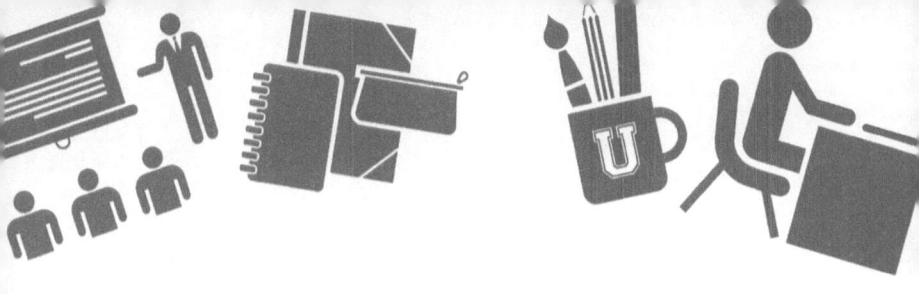

TABLE OF CONTENTS

1	. . . .	61
2	. . . .	77
3	. . . .	79
4	. . . .	83

1

William Tucker leaves the office of Dr. Jacoby, trying to hide his semi-erection with his book bag as he walks down the corridor, relieved that no other students are around. It's early evening, and the building is often empty at this time. Only professors are still lingering in their offices, catching up on grading or whatever else it is they do when they aren't teaching.

He tries to ignore the image that forms in his mind of Dr. Jacoby alone in her office after hours, hair unbound and free as she stretches in her desk chair, the shape of her full breasts revealed as her shirt tightens, long shapely legs on display as she rests her bare feet on the desk in front of her. He knows that she has started wearing stockings lately, likely garters if the quick glimpse he'd seen when he'd once walked into her office unannounced to find her slightly sprawled in the chair before she quickly rearranged her legs to hide her thighs was accurate, but at the start of the semester, she'd been prone to bare legs, and he knows she takes her shoes off under the desk every chance she gets.

He likes Dr. Jacoby, but it's an idle fantasy—she's never looked at him with true desire. He has a feeling that she has a lover and a truly wild side, but it's mostly conjecture, and though he enjoys toying with the idea, he enjoys his discussions with her far more.

His slightly hard dick is more a result of the lack of action lately than any actual lust.

Reaching the end of the hallway, William looks from the door to the stairwell on his right to the elevator doors on his left. He can take the elevator down the four floors to the ground, but he's heard that alarm go off more than once while in class, and he's also heard his fellow students complain about how often it breaks down—and just how long it has taken for someone to show up and open those doors. He shivers at the thought of being stuck in there all night long.

Unless Dr. Jacoby discovered him and he hit the porn lottery, it would be a lonely experience. Though he has never had sex in an elevator before, he tries to shut down the part of his mind that wonders at the logistics. There was that bar that ran around the inside about hip level—could he wedge her on top of that and stand up? He might be the right height, but he doesn't want to end up doing the splits while fucking her—his thighs aren't up to that kind of exercise for any extended period of time. He's not in awful shape, but he's no athlete either. He doesn't want to lay her on the floor either, not after so many people have been doing who-knows-what in there all day. The idea of sitting naked on the floor douses any remaining desire, and he lets his mind wander in another direction.

He wonders who would miss him if he didn't go home tonight, and then tries not to think about that either. He pictures the empty apartment waiting for him and decides that he can't face it right now. Not yet. He's been lingering in his professor's office, finding reasons to stay and chat so he doesn't have to think about the empty side of the closet where all of his ex's clothes used to hang, the empty spaces in his bathroom where she used to keep all of her stuff. And how much stuff it had been—who knew how much shit women needed to get ready? He decides that he doesn't mind having his bathroom sink to himself again. The rest, though, still stings.

I can't go home right now, William decides, checking his watch to see if the library is still open. 7:30. Another half hour. That will work for a bit, he decides, and then maybe he will go to the diner across the street and do some classwork until he gets tired and can't think anymore.

Plan in mind, he heads down the stairs, trotting down all four flights easily, his boots echoing loudly in the empty stairwell. He reaches the bottom, erection forgotten, mind already cataloguing the chapters he will read first, and opens the heavy outside door to the breezeway between this building and the library when he collides with another person. There is a crash of bodies, a flutter of papers and books that scatter around them, and a decidedly frustrated female curse.

William looks up, taking in the flowered dress surrounding luscious curves, the horn-rimmed glasses before bright eyes, the dark hair secured in a bun but with wisps escaping to frame a lovely face. "I'm so sorry!" he exclaims, pushing the door out again as it starts to close on both of them. "I didn't see you," he adds lamely.

The woman looks at him, then at the pile of papers and books laying haphazardly around them. One of the pages starts to blow away in the breeze from the open door, and without thinking, William steps on it to keep it in place. She sighs, the sound an echo of the tiredness in William's soul, and he grins at her in understanding. He is mildly surprised when she grins back. His experiences with women have taught him to expect annoyance or frustration—definitely not this shared camaraderie.

"No worries," she says in a friendly voice, pushing by him and allowing the door to close. She leans down to start gathering the papers and books, and William bends down to help. He moves his foot off the piece of paper and reaches down, and as he does, she leans forward, and the two of them clunk foreheads with a loud hollow sound.

The collision causes both of them to sit back hard on their heels and eventually fall onto their butts. William's first impulse is to laugh, and the sound escapes him without warning, but then she is laughing, and then they are staring at each other through a haze of pain and tears as the laughter tears through them. When they finally collect themselves, William is trying not to be so obvious in checking out the length of pale thigh exposed by her dress, the floral material currently riding high on her lap. She seems to follow his gaze, but instead of glaring at him, she smiles, the expression warming her face and matching her cheeks, still pink from laughter.

They sit there for another companionable moment, and then she sighs heavily, the sound loud in the empty stairwell, surveying the mass of paper and books around them. "Let me help you with that," William offers, reaching out slowly to collect the closest papers. He glances at them as he does so, surprised to discover they are not student essays as he had thought. The writing is double-spaced, but there are no headings to mark student names. A line from the text jumps out at him:

"Please," she screamed, "Please fuck me!"

Intrigued, William lets his eyes wander along the page, at first sure he is tired and misreading things, but then she is grabbing for the pages, and their hands meet, and she is looking at him and he is looking at her, each waiting for the other to speak. William takes the plunge.

"Interesting reading material," he comments, sliding the pages into a pile without reading further.

She quirks an eyebrow at him, again, not the expected reaction. If he'd been reading porn and someone busted him, he did not think he'd be able to sit there so calmly. She shrugs, one delicate shoulder raising, her flowered dress tightening against the line of her breast, her white sweater lifting and falling with a soft whisper of sound. "It gets boring just sitting there. I thought I'd spice it up."

He hands her the pile, noticing how her fingers trail along his as she takes it from him, then stacks it on top of one of the books she has gathered. "Sitting where?" he asks, hoping the moment will last, wishing to spend more time with this curious creature sitting across from him.

She gives him a considering look, and he sees the moment when she decides to trust him. "The Tutoring Center," she says. "It's a ghost town over there after 5 o'clock. I mostly just sit and read all evening."

"Really?" William asks. "I've seen some people over there at night..." He trails off, berating himself for contradicting her. She works there, he tells himself, surely she knows better than he does.

Again, that shrug. "Sometimes, sure, especially the football team around midterms, but right now? Dead zone." She scoots back, preparing to stand up. "I need something to read or I will fall asleep."

"Do you always read ... such material?" he asks.

She gives him a naughty grin, a look all promise that makes him want to see her with her hair down, with that sweater on the floor, with that dress around her waist. "Sometimes," she replies. "A girl has to keep herself entertained."

"I would love to entertain you," he says, the words out before he can stop them, and he stares at her, thinking that surely he has gone too far, that she will call him a creep and walk away.

But the tutor does none of those things. Instead, she looks excited, eyes wide, breath slightly fast, a slow flush of red creeping up her chest. "How would you entertain me?" she breathes, and then he is crawling toward her, fallen books forgotten, and he lifts one of her hands from the pile she holds, raises it to his lips in an oddly gallant gesture, and releases it.

"Believe me," he tells her, "I could think of a few things."

She looks from her hand to his mouth and back again, and William knows she was expecting him to kiss her just then. She doesn't try to run away, a good sign, but he doesn't want to push it too far right now. But then, she speaks, and his doubts fade away.

"Would you show me some of those things?" she asks, moving to her knees and creeping closer, scattered papers forgotten beneath her. William doesn't miss the invitation in her voice.

"Oh yes," he promises, reaching for her hand again. "First," he says, "I would take your hand and kiss it." His lips are soft against her palm as he kisses it, his breath warm against her skin as he speaks, "And then I would move up your arm, tasting your skin." She shivers as he does as he says, his mouth moving slowly up the inside of her arm, soft butterfly kisses on the inside of her wrist and then up to her elbow as he pushes her sweater up before him.

She sighs, skin prickling in response to his touch. Moving his face away from her arm, he slowly reaches for her neck, sliding the sweater down off her shoulder so it hangs on her elbow and around her back.

"Then I would kiss you here," he announces, moving in slowly to trace his mouth along the line of her neck and shoulder, crossing the thin material of her dress's shoulder strap, noting that she isn't wearing a bra underneath, or if she is, it does not have straps. He slides his other hand up her opposite side under her sweater, pausing to stroke the sensitive skin near her breasts through the thin fabric of her dress. "And I would touch you there."

A breathy sound escapes her as his mouth reaches the top of her arm and his hand reaches up to stroke the curve of her breast. He pauses, enjoying the sensations, letting the moment linger, then pulls slowly away from her shoulder, leaving his hand resting under her breast. "And then I would pause, to see what you wanted next."

She is looking at him, something between wonder and desire in her expression, and William smiles at her. He knows that his methods of seduction aren't for everyone, but this woman seems to be enjoying everything.

"Next," she says, the word shaping her lips as she purses them for the sound, "you want to know what I want." Her eyes scan his face, lingering on his mouth. "I want you to tell me more."

He smiles at her, eyes narrowing playfully, and he leans forward again, left hand moving up to cover her breast, fingers circling her nipple, feeling it harden beneath his touch, "I would touch you here, loving the feel of you." He runs his other hand over her right shoulder, fingers sliding the strap of her dress down over her arm, the front of the dress following. His left hand abandons her nipple for a moment, mimicking the movement of his right hand and sliding her sweater and strap down to the crook of her elbow.

"And then I would admire your breasts," he narrates, gently tugging the forgiving material of the dress down and scooping out both of her breasts so they rest on top of the former neckline. He bends down to take a nipple in his mouth, and she gasps, leaning back and bracing herself with her palms on the floor behind her. "I would suck your nipples," he breathes against her, the warmth of his breath teasing her wet skin and causing her nipples to harden even more.

"Yes," she moans, lifting one hand to press his head against her breasts, fingers twining in his hair. He sucks for a long moment, moving from one nipple to the other, dexterous fingers replacing his mouth and stroking her sensitive skin. Her hands tighten in his hair, and she tugs him away, eyes dark with desire. "Then what?" she asks, voice undercut with a hint of command.

He pushes her back gently, his legs prodding between her thighs as he inches forward on his knees. She obliges, opening her legs to let him between them, but also scooting slowly backwards. "Then I would kiss you," he tells her, one hand still on her body as he moves her across the floor, the other sliding up her arm to her neck and in her hair, his face even with hers as his lips meet hers in a soft kiss. He is gentle, but firm, lips moving against hers in a way that is all promise.

When she opens her mouth, his tongue slides against hers, taking in her warmth and lingering in all the right places. The hand on her body holds her close, his knees still inching her backwards, and then her feet hit something. She opens her eyes, seeming surprised to see the bottom step behind her as she glances back. William uses the momentary distraction to put both hands on her hips and lift her onto the step. He scoots in close, kissing her again, both hands exploring the curves of her body, the soft material of her dress tantalizing under his fingers.

When they pause for breath, he lifts her up again, this time moving her up two steps, so she is sitting above him. "Then I would touch your thighs," he tells her, moving his hands to the outside of her thighs, slipping under her dress and scooting the material up. Her legs are lovely, smooth and toned, and she shivers as he reaches the top, hands cradling her hips, the flowered dress bunched up to reveal white cotton panties.

She leans back, elbows on the step behind her, and looks down the length of her body at him, her exposed breasts resting on top of the dress, nipples hard.

"And then I would want to see all of you," he explains, "so I would slide these off." His fingers begin the agonizingly slow work of removing her panties. She watches him as her flesh is revealed, breasts heaving as she breathes, a flush working its way up her neck. He tugs the panties down and over the white sandals, then tucks them into his pocket, not wanting to put them on the floor of the stairwell. He touches her feet, then runs his hands up her calves, dipping behind her knees and then between her thighs, spreading them apart as he leans forward even more.

"I would watch your face as I touched you," he says as his hands slide across her skin, "here," and then as his thumb reaches the swollen nub of her clit, "and here."

She gasps, head falling back as he gently presses, then she is looking at him, biting her lower lip as he strokes her skin, slow luscious circles with his thumb, and then his other hand is sliding lower, fingers tracing the edges of her smooth skin before sliding slowly inside her, her warm wetness plump with desire. Her eyes narrow in pleasure, but she doesn't look away, doesn't lose herself in the sensation yet. William's hands continue to move in a slow delicious rhythm, and her hips begin to move against him, gently urging him along.

"I would want to see you come for me," he says, thumb moving faster against her clit, and she rocks herself against him, a low moan spilling from her lips. "So I would rub right there," he describes, "and press here," as his hands move in tandem, her hips moving faster against him, her breasts bouncing as she slides closer to orgasm.

"Will you come for me?" he asks, and then he is up on his knees again, lips finding hers without losing the rhythm of both hands, and as his tongue finds hers, she shudders against him, a moan lost inside his mouth, and he lets his hands slow, but does not move them away. "Yes," he whispers against her open mouth, "that's what I would do." He moves his face away for a moment, allowing her to catch her breath, then adds, "But I would not be finished after one orgasm."

She regains her breath and her composure, her expression satisfied but curious. "No?" she asks, a hand brushing loose strands of hair out of her face, her bun coming loose. "What would you do next?"

He leans back, then scoots down, sitting on his folded legs, and slowly moves his hands around, enjoying the small gasps of pleasure escaping her. He settles his face against her knee, kissing the skin of her inner thigh, then moving up.

"I would need to know what you taste like," he says, using both hands to press her thighs wide, "so I would kiss you here." He presses his lips to her clit, sucking quickly and releasing her as her hips jerk forward. One hand slides down and slips inside her again, not moving, but pressing against her from the inside.

"Then I would want to feel you," he whispers against her skin, "and lick you." His tongue runs along the length of her, starting near his finger inside her and ending on her clit and lingering. She shudders against him, and his other hand reaches around her hips and settles under her ass, holding her steady so she can't move too far from him.

"I would want to hear what you want," he orders, then licks her again, finger joined by another inside her as he starts another slow rhythm.

She says nothing for a moment, but then he pauses, looking up at her. His tongue darts out for a quick lick, then retreats. "I would want to know if you wanted me to do this," a longer luscious lick from top to bottom, "or this," and a final long suck that has her head sink limply back and her thighs begin to tremble, "or maybe this."

"Yes," she breathes.

Another long suckling where his tongue presses hard against her as his fingers continue to move inside her. "Yes what?"

"Yes that!" she says, voice slightly louder. "That is so fucking good!"

"What is so fucking good?" he asks, warm breath close, fingers still moving in that maddening rhythm. "Tell me."

"I want you to suck my clit!" she semi-yells, the words echoing in the empty stairwell. "Then I want you to fuck me!"

"Fuck you?" he asks, sucking her again until she shudders. "How will I fuck you?" He sucks again, fingers sliding in and out of her, and her hips are pumping up and down on his hand. "Tell me how!"

"Hard!" she yells, body lost in pleasure as she rocks on his hand, and he sucks again, this time not releasing her until she tenses, entire body taut with the power of her orgasm. "Fuck me hard," she moans as she comes, "make me come on your dick. I need you inside of me!"

She falls back, collapsing on the stairs, and he uses the moment to remove his hands, unzipping his pants and pulling out his hard cock. He sits up, knees still on the ground but his body even with hers, pressing the tip of his cock against her wet opening. "Look at me," he commands. "I want you to watch me fuck you."

Her eyes open slowly, and her head comes back up, but then is looking at his cock in his hand pressed between her thighs, and she bites her lip again, and her body slides down a little, eager to have him inside of her. "You want this cock?" he asks, rubbing himself against her, her wetness combining with his pre-cum to create delightful friction. "You want this inside you?"

"Yes!" she says, one arm reaching forward to grab him, pressing herself forward. "I want you inside me!" Her hand reaches behind him as she sits up slightly, fingers grabbing his ass and pulling him closer.

He allows himself to be moved, the tip of his cock sliding into that delicious warmth. He pauses, then pulls back, slipping in and out slowly. "Like that?" he asks, one hand grabbing her hip and holding her where he wants her, the other reaching up to caress her breast, rubbing her nipple with his thumb.

The hand on his ass tightens, and then she is sitting up on the step, her other hand grabbing his hips, and she presses herself onto him, his cock sliding in deep. She sighs, "Fuck yes," and scoots forward, trying to get traction, her legs wrapping around his hips and tugging him closer. He leans toward her, capturing her mouth with his, letting her taste herself on his lips, her tongue pressing into his mouth as he slides his hips slowly back and forth. "More," she pleads into his mouth. "I need more!"

His hand abandons her breast, joining the other on her hips, and he tugs her close, giving her the connection she wants. Now more balanced, she presses herself into him, and he grips her hips hard, yanking her against him, his cock plunging deep inside her warmth. "Yes!" she yells.

He moves her again, using his position to tuck himself underneath her, his hands rocking her hips as he dives in and out of her. He feels her start to tighten even more around his cock, "And then I would watch you come on my cock!" he yells, and she opens her eyes as she comes, body shuddering in ecstasy.

After a moment, she slows her movement, some of the desperation leaving her, and a new wildness seems to fill her. She sits up, allowing his cock to retreat a little, then releases her legs from his hips.

"And then I would make you sit down," she tells him, pulling away and scooting aside so that he can sit on the vacated step. He does so, turning around so he sits on the step instead of her. "And I would take these off," she says, kneeling before him to tug off his pants and boxers. They tangle around his ankles, but she doesn't try to get them passed his boots, leaving them there and standing up, glorious body before him as she turns around, shucking off the forgotten sweater in one angry motion and lowering herself onto him, her legs pressing his knees together as she sits on his lap, her back to him. He leans back on the step, resting on his elbows as she did before, then watches as she lowers a most perfect ass before his sight, her warmth embracing his hard cock as she takes him inside, and after a moment where she adjusts her feet on either side of him, and presses her hands against the tops of his thighs for balance, she lifts herself slowly up and down on him.

"And then I would ride his cock until I came again!" she says, the words triumphant as she finds her rhythm, beautiful ass pounding up and down as she moves. William is enthralled, but doesn't want to lose himself in the moment, not yet, so he reaches up with one hand and grips her hip, following the rhythm she sets for a moment, before sliding his hand around and down to stroke her clit with his thumb.

"And I would rub that sweet clit until you came on my cock," he groans, trying to slow the inexorable build of pleasure spiking through him. "Come for me, baby," he demands, "Come now!"

He rubs harder, faster, and she shudders on him, hands gripping his thighs in spasms as the orgasm rocks her. She slumps then, leaning back against him, gasping for breath, sweat coating her neck. He sits up, pressing her back to him, and uses the break to slide her dress up and over her head. She allows the movement, hand reaching up lazily to adjust her glasses where they are askew on her face, resting limply against him, and then he is rubbing her breasts, slowly, but determined, and she moves, the slight motion pressing him deep inside her again as her muscles relax. His hands wander down, and he reaches her clit again, exerting gentle pressure when she stiffens against him, clearly needing a moment, and slipping down to feel himself inside of her. She shudders, a low spasm of pleasure, as his fingers caress her skin around his cock, and then he is kissing her neck. She turns her head, and then she is kissing him, and she moves ever so gently, rocking slowly up and down on his cock.

"Then I would fuck you slow until you screamed my name," he says against her lips, and she pauses, eyes opening to look at him.

"But I don't know your name," she says, a bit of a giggle escaping as she moved up and down on his cock.

"William Turner," he growls, and moves both hands to her hips to keep her moving at the current rhythm, pleasure building again inside him, and this time he doesn't want to stop, "and don't you ever forget it."

She moves on him faster, still not the frantic rhythm of a few moments before, but definitely on her way to another orgasm. "I will never forget your name, William Turner," she moans, eyes closing as the pleasure builds in her.

"And your name?" he asks, trying to slow the moment, but aware that he is going to lose himself and soon. Slow steady rhythms always undo him. "What name will I dream about tonight?"

"Kimberly," she answers, then kisses him again, slow and languorous. "Kimberly Chapman."

His hands press hard against her hips, setting the rhythm, "I would tell you how lovely you are, Kimberly Chapman," he says, loving the feel of her name on his lips, and then she kisses him again, both of them lost in pleasure.

William is about to lose himself completely, but a sound echoes through his concentration, breaking his rhythm and coordination, and he opens his eyes to meet Kimberly's stunned expression as her brain processes the noise. The door has opened in the stairwell, probably not on the second floor because it sounds farther away, but definitely marking the arrival of someone else in the building.

Kimberly stands up quickly, reaching for her discarded dress and sweater and clutching them to her chest, eyes wide and hair wild as she takes in the sprawl of papers and books abandoned on the floor. William stands, nearly tumbles as his pants catch around his ankles, and then yanks them up awkwardly. Kimberly bends down and starts collecting the papers, but William stops her with a gesture, motioning to the books instead. She begins gathering them, deciding to abandon the pages, and William helps, clutching three books against his chest with one hand and the other holding his pants up. She looks at the door, then down at her clothes, and he can see the indecision in her eyes.

It's one thing to abandon papers with no names on it; it's another to run outside completely naked. It's late in the evening, but the college isn't completely deserted.

William makes a snap decision, gestures for her to follow, and darts farther into the stairwell, ducking underneath the space created by the stairs. Most of the school stairwells use the space for storage, and this stairwell is no exception, the space occupied with blue gym mats stacked both horizontally and vertically. There is a space against the wall wide enough for them to fit inside, and William shoos Kimberly in ahead of him, using his body to block the opening in case the person decides to come back here. Kimberly lets the books in one hand tumble to the surface of a pile of horizontal mats about chest high, the sound a low thud that seems very loud in the echoing stairwell, and William sets his down with more grace. She is tugging her dress over her head, arms akimbo as the twisted material gets stuck, and he reaches out to help her. Both of them freeze as they hear footsteps on the stairs above their heads. Without thought, he lifts her up onto the mats and scoots up behind her.

They hear a soft curse in Spanish as the person comes down the stairs, no doubt taking in the spray of abandoned papers, and then there is some shuffling. William wonders if it could be the janitor; he doesn't think another student would bother to pick up the papers.

Kimberly is kneeling in front of him, head barely peeking over the vertical mats piled in front of the ones they are on, her body faintly outlined in the dim light, and William can't help the way his dick hardens again, danger momentarily forgotten. Her head cocks to the side, hair mussed and bun lost as she listens to the person on the other side of the steps.

The shuffling sounds continue for a moment, and William scoots closer to her, allowing his pants to fall down around his thighs as he presses himself against her. She gasps, and there is a pause in the sounds outside, then her hands are reaching behind her, fingers grabbing his hard cock and pressing it. She turns around, her mouth open in shock but something naughty crossing her face. William moves his hips forward, cock angling for her opening, and she grins at him over her shoulder, opening her legs to let him in.

He hovers at her entrance for a moment, straining to hear the person on the other side of the stairs, but also so blue-balled that he really doesn't care much about what they do over there. The shuffling continues, papers being collected, and he inches forward, cock slipping inside of velvety heat one slow inch at a time. Kimberly lets out a slow ragged breath, and reaches back to grab his hand where it rests on her ass. He pulls out slowly, letting the friction build, and then slides back inside. Her other hand reaches around behind her, and then she is gripping both of his hands where they hold her ass, letting him set the rhythm.

He moves a few more times, tension building, and the person continues to collect papers. There is more shuffling, the sound of a random pile of papers being tapped into a pile, and then a cough and another Spanish curse.

William pauses, wondering if the person had heard them, but then there is a soft chuckle from the other side of the stairs, and more shuffling as the person rearranges the papers. A soft thud lets them know that the newcomer has decided to sit down on the stairs, a soft sliding of paper against paper letting them know the person is reading the discarded papers. William holds in a laugh, unable to quite believe the situation. An hour ago, he never would have guessed that he'd be hiding under a staircase with his dick buried in the hottest woman he'd ever met with a stranger reading porn a few feet away.

He allows himself to move again, ever so slowly, and Kimberly moves with him, as caught up in the moment as he is. A few more soft strokes, and then there is a chuckle from the stranger. He doesn't pause, the slow motion of his cock inside her sweet pussy driving him mad. Another few chuckles, and then another sound, one he recognizes, an intrigued noise.

There is another shift as the newcomer turns to the next page, and then the unmistakable sound of a zipper. William doesn't stop, but doesn't speed up either, knowing both he and Kimberly are intently listening to the stranger on the steps. More paper shuffling, and then something that could be clothing shuffling, and then the unmistakable slow fapping sound of a man masturbating. Kimberly doesn't turn around, and William is grateful for that, knowing they would both lose it if they looked at one another right now. Instead he continues to slowly slide in and out of her, careful not to move too quickly so their bodies don't make any noise.

Kimberly is so wet and tight that he knows he isn't going to last much longer. The sound of the fapping gets more intense, and they can hear labored breathing as another paper shuffles. Then, there is a moan, and a hand slaps against the stairs above them, and Kimberly's pussy squeezes tight around him, her body shuddering. William's entire body convulses, and he comes, not hard as he had first imagined, but slow and agonizing and sweet, pumping at the same speed a few more times until the moment passes, and he falls back on his haunches, Kimberly following him to sit on his lap, his cock still buried inside of her.

William takes long slow breaths, feeling his heart pounding in his head, the feeling oddly echoed by Kimberly's own pulse beating against him as she sprawls against him. They don't move, listening for the newcomer.

After a moment, the breathing slows, and then there is the shuffling of clothing and the zipper again. The papers are shuffled, there is a cough, and then the exterior door opens and footsteps walk through. The door bangs shut, and Kimberly turns in the circle of William's arms, staring at him. They both look at one another for a long moment, and then dissolve into fits of wheezing giggles, the movement pushing him out of her as his body tightens.

When they have calmed down a little bit, Kimberly scoots away, rolling over to sit on the mat a foot away from him. "Well," she says finally, "that was definitely entertaining."

Williams grins at her, then scoots to the edge of the mat and slides his pants back up as he jumps off, taking the time to actually zip and button them before reaching out a hand to help Kimberly climb down. They both grab her books, and creep out from behind the mats.

William holds her books as she shrugs into her sweater and rearranges her hair, massing it back into a bun in a way that makes William want to take it down again. She gives him a look as if asking how she looks, and he nods at her. She looks wonderful, skin rosy with the aftereffects of good sex, and now that he knows what is underneath that dress, he is tempted to take it off of her again.

He looks around at the stairwell, then down at himself. She considers, then steps forward and smooths his hair before she nods, giving him the same approval to go out in public. She lands a soft kiss on his lips that turns into something more, and they linger there in the stairwell next to the mats, not caring if someone walks in on them kissing.

After a long moment, they pause, and Kimberly looks at him. "What do you say we go grab a cup of coffee and get to know one another? It's far too early to go home yet."

William nods. "I know a great diner right around the corner."

2

"*A*re you a writer, William?" Kimberly asks, eyes dark and inviting over the mug of coffee. They have been talking for about an hour, getting to know one another in other ways.

He shrugs, looking at his own empty mug on the table, then decides to own it. She could hardly be surprised, given the way he had just made love to her. She had to know he loved words. "Yeah," he admits, then remembers her voice shouting in the stairwell, body flushed with desire for him, and says it again, stronger this time. "Yes, I'm a writer."

"What do you write?" she asks, her voice a low purr.

He shrugs again, then looks down again, knowing what he should expect her expression to do when he says it, knowing how women normally respond to him, but hoping this time will be different, that she will be different. She already is different. He tries to shake the nagging sense of inevitability that lingers. Kimberly isn't like the other women he's known. She isn't going to react the way he expects. "I write about ... life," he admits.

She leans in, face curious, and a rush of excitement fills William's chest. "What about life?" The words are nearly a whisper now. "Do you write about what just happened?"

"Not usually," he tells her, thinking about his few attempts at erotica, "but I could write something for you." He looks up, thinking of her alone in the Tutoring Center after hours, reading his words. "Just for you." He cocks his head, biting his lower lip. "Would you read it?"

She considers, a small smile playing on her lips. "That depends. Would it be worth reading?"

He nods, and confidence fills him. He knows how to use words. "I think I could keep your attention," he teases. "Perhaps you'd enjoy it as much as the janitor." She giggles, and he reaches out to take her hand. "What kind of story would you like to read?"

She ponders for a moment, then tilts her head, bun gone, all that long dark hair sliding over her shoulders and caressing her upper arms, bare now that she's removed her sweater. "How about a story about life?" she replies with a smirk.

"Life," he repeats, ideas spinning in his head, "like real life … or something else?"

She looks around. "Well, I have a real life, so something else would probably keep my attention more effectively," she breathes.

William nods, a plot already forming as he stares at her, taking in her small mannerisms, her gestures, her expressions. He knows he can capture her in fiction. "I can bring it to you tomorrow," he offers.

"Tomorrow night?" she clarifies. "I'm closing the Tutoring Center, so I'll be there alone after 6."

"Sounds perfect," he says.

"Awesome," she says, "now let's talk about my panties still in your pocket."

3

*W*illiam stands in front of the elevator with Kimberly, waiting for the doors to open. He is a little bit nervous to get in the contraption, especially considering what he knows about the elevator in the Humanities Building, but he's willing to risk it to spend a few more minutes with her.

Kimberly needs a few things from the Tutoring Center before she heads home for the night. She hadn't planned on leaving when she bumped into him in the stairwell; she had just been running over to the mailroom before heading back to the Tutoring Center. Now it is very late, and the Center is closed, so she has to remove the sign that she left hours earlier, the one that lied, saying "Be back in five minutes." She hopes no students waited for any real length of time. She really had meant to be right back; she hadn't expected to bump into William in the stairwell and get completely distracted.

"It's fine," she tells William as the doors slide open. "I use this elevator all the time."

"I know," William admits, but he can't shake the feeling he has that he is about to get stuck in an elevator.

She grabs his hand and leads him inside, leaning down to press the button for the fourth floor. The elevator moves slowly, but steadily up, each floor marked by a low ding. William is staring at the doors, face nervous, so Kimberly leans in to him, propping her books in one arm and tugging his face down to kiss her. He seems to enjoy the distraction, soft lips pressing against hers. He focuses, adjusting the books he carries for her so he has a free arm to wrap around her back, and runs a hand up her spine. She shivers in his embrace.

The elevator stops on the fourth floor with a ding, and the doors slide open. William finishes kissing her, and steps back, clearly expecting her to lead him out of the elevator, but instead, she takes the pile of books in his arm, adds it to her own, and places it in the corner. The doors stay open for a moment and then begin to slide shut. William starts to say something, but then Kimberly has both hands in his hair, tugging him down to kiss her again, and the words die on his tongue. Both of his hands come around her back and slide down to cup her ass, and she bites his lip a little.

The door has shut completely, but the elevator hasn't moved. William realizes that it won't move until someone else calls it to a different floor, or someone on the fourth floor pushes the button. He's seen the dark offices along the hallway leading to the library and he doesn't think anyone will be using this elevator any time soon.

Then again, he'd had the same thought about the stairs earlier tonight. But that had been a janitor. Not that janitors wouldn't use the elevator—they often do to move the carts—but anyone would have to call the elevator down to the bottom. It doesn't move fast; they will have a chance to get themselves presentable again.

Besides, Kimberly is pressing herself against him and he knows that she isn't wearing panties, and he slides his hands beneath her dress to feel the slick wetness between her thighs. She turns so her back is against the wall, and then he pushes himself against her, wondering just how he's going to fuck her in this elevator. He wants to speak, to say something, knowing that words turn her on, but there is an odd silence between them, a connection purely physical, and he just wants the moment to last.

Kimberly reaches down and starts undoing his pants, dexterous fingers unfastening the button and lowering the zipper, and then his hard cock is in her hands, and she is stroking him. She releases him for a moment, her hand slipping beneath her dress to touch her own wetness, and then she is sliding her smooth hands over his cock, the friction a promise of pleasures to come. He kisses her again, tugging her hair down and pressing her against the wall. There is a railing that runs around the middle of the elevator, and William wonders if she can rest on it to get her at a better angle.

She seems to read his mind because she hops up, resting the edge of her ass on the edge of the railing, and spreads her legs welcomingly. William presses himself between them, his weight holding her steady on the railing, a hand under her ass to hold her in place, and then her hand is guiding him into her wetness, the tip slipping inside and then she moans as he fills her completely, the sensation of warmth and tightness multiplied by the feeling of her fingers still wrapped around him, sliding up and down as he presses his length into her and rocks back out again. She uses her other hand to grip his shoulder hard, balancing against the wall and rocking softly up and down on his cock. Her legs wrap around his hips, urging him deeper.

He moans, setting a slow luscious pace, boots getting excellent traction on the elevator floor, and loses himself in the moment. The only sound is their panting breath, the noise of their bodies fitting together, a wet slapping that, after the evening filled with words, only turns him on more. Words are well and good, but there is something to be said for good old fashioned fucking. Kimberly's hand continues to slide against him as he fucks her, a lovely sensation against his cock, her fingers pressing against her clit in a rhythm that grows slightly faster as he moves. She moans, the sound lost in his mouth, and he devours her with his mouth, one hand holding her firmly under her ass and the other holding her chin as he rocks on his heels.

He speeds up, suddenly wanting to come again, and then she is biting his lips as she kisses him, her hand on his shoulder digging in as she moves faster, body pounding up and down harder, breasts bouncing wildly against his chest. He puts a hand against the wall to brace himself, fingers digging into her ass and putting her at the perfect angle, and then he lets go completely, pounding into her until the orgasm hits, letting his body freeze as he comes into her, then gasping in ragged breaths as she shudders against him, finding her own pleasure just before he steps back, light-headed and weak-kneed, and then she slides down off the railing onto shaky legs.

They both stand there for a moment, Kimberly gripping the railing behind her with both hands, gasping and flushed, and William leans back against the closed doors, heart pounding like mad and eyes glazed with the residue of lust. After a moment, William adjusts his pants, tucking himself back inside and zipping up. Kimberly's dress has already fallen back into place.

He follows her gaze as her eyes linger on his pocket, and he tucks the exposed edge of her panties back inside, shaking his head with a grin. She raises an eyebrow, but says nothing.

There is another long moment filled only with their slowing breaths, and then they look at one another again. Kimberly steps away from the wall and William steps away from the door, and they meet in the middle of the elevator for another kiss, lips moving slowly against one another, exploring, comforting, loving.

It is a long time before the elevator doors open again.

4

Kimberly Chapman waits in the Tutoring Center, trying not to watch the clock as the minutes tick by. The computer monitor before her is loaded with numbers, formulas she should be reviewing since the football team would be in tomorrow to prepare for their algebra midterm, but Kimberly doesn't need to study; she could tutor algebra in her sleep. But the numbers have been a distraction, and one her boss would approve of, if Dianne Carver ever actually came in the Center at night. But no one has even been there to see her fake brushing up, and now she gives up completely.

The clock says 5:58. She wonders how prompt William Turner will be, excited by the thought of seeing him, of hopefully getting to slide that glorious cock inside her again, intrigued by the story he had promised to write her. Her hand slides down the black dress she wears, lingers on her knee, and then wanders underneath the dress and slides along her inner thigh. Thoughts of William's words, then his mouth on her, then his cock inside her, the rush of the frantic elevator sex, and soon she is stroking herself, finger deftly rubbing her clit, glad she left the panties at home today.

She watches the glass doorway between this room and the hallway, knowing that the library on the other end of the hallway still has clusters of students, but sure that none of them will come to the Center this late. She hadn't been kidding when she told William the place is a Dead Zone after five o'clock.

Her finger moves again at the thought of William, and she glances first at the clock and then at the door. It really wouldn't do to have him walk in on her fingering herself. Then again, she considers the look that would cross his face, and wonders what naughty words he would say, and her finger moves faster, low heat building in her belly.

Motion in the hallway catches her attention and she pulls her hand out from under her dress, sliding the chair forward so she is nearly under the desk, attention clearly focused on the monitor when the door opens.

William is just as handsome as he was the night before, his upper body covered by a button-down shirt that doesn't quite hide the definition of his muscles. He's not a large man, not at all, but he's fit and toned enough to make her want to run her hands along his chest, kissing her way down the muscles of his stomach and lower. He takes in the empty room and her desk in the far corner. Kimberly's face lights in a smile, and William returns the look.

"You looking for some help?" she asks jokingly.

"Maybe," he replies, crossing the room, walking passed computers and a few cubicles in the center to stand before her L-shaped desk. "I was told someone here might be looking for some entertainment."

Kimberly spins her chair slightly to face him directly and leans back. She watches William take in the simple black dress that can't hide her curves, the skirt modestly covering her knees and falling mid-calf but revealing the small black sandals on her feet. She lifts one leg and crosses it over the other, the motion hopefully slow enough for him to guess that she isn't wearing panties. "Maybe," she says. "Depends on what you mean by entertainment."

William grins as he watches her legs move. "Well, well," he observes in a low voice that sends a shiver across her skin, "you seem to have left some clothing at home today."

She nods, a smirk in her voice. "You wouldn't believe what happened."

"Try me," he says, putting down his bag on the chair and leaning on the edge of the desk.

She uncrosses her legs and spreads them, scooting the hem of the dress up her thighs. "Someone seems to have taken my panties," she says quietly, a little pout on her lips.

"Really? How upsetting," he comments, glancing out the glass door to the empty hallway beyond. He slides his legs up and over the desk, so he leans on her side now, and then he sinks to his knees before her chair. "I think I might have to investigate further."

"Would you?" she asks, and her legs open a little bit more. William scoots forward, accepting the invitation, and his hands slide up the outside of her thighs, causing chills to run through her at his touch. He pauses at her bare hips, then slides both hands lower and between her thighs, stroking the warm heat there. "And what do you think?" she asks, eyes dark with desire.

"I think I may have to explore the issue," he tells her, sinking down so he cannot be seen beneath the desk, and he tugs the chair toward him, burying his face between her thighs under her dress.

Kimberly gasps, pleasure flooding her as his mouth closes over her clit, tongue sucking in the way he knows she likes. One hand slips down to stroke her pussy low and slow, but the other creeps up underneath her dress to cup her breast, thumb sliding across the nipple. Kimberly whimpers, the sound loud in the empty room, and she watches the door, glad that no one is there. "Oh yes," she whispers, one hand pressing against the back of William's head under her dress, pushing him into her, and the other reaching up to caress her other breast, rubbing one nipple as he rubs the other. "You can keep exploring all day."

William reaches down and tugs her forward on the chair, exposing more of her flesh to his hands and mouth, and she puts both hands on the back of his head, forgetting about the glass door, forgetting about everything but the motion of his mouth on her skin, the pulsing building heat in her lower belly. Both of his hands slide between her legs, and his fingers begin that magical motion in conjunction with his tongue. Already excited from the few moments before he arrived, Kimberly comes quickly, the orgasm hard as her pulse echoes in her fingertips, her fingers white from where she's been pressing them against William's head. She releases him, letting her body slide down in the chair, pleasure rendering her muscles limp with fatigue.

William sits up, giving her space, and surveys her. "I've been waiting to taste you all day," he says, running a hand along his lips.

Regaining her head, Kimberly opens an eye. "I thought you were writing all day?"

He nods. "I was, and that's why I couldn't wait to see you." He climbs to his knees and stands up, easily sliding back over the desk to his bag. He opens it, then slides out a blue folder with a small stack of papers inside. He lays it on the desk, then slides it toward her.

"And in a folder!" she exclaims, eyes meeting his, no doubt recalling the explosion of loose papers that had brought them together in the stairwell. Kimberly leans forward to take it, smiling at him as she flips it open. She removes the pages and lays them on top of the folder, biting her lip as she begins to scan the words.

"Oh no," he says, and she pauses, looking up at him, eyes already hooded with desire. "Not like that," he tells her. "Read it out loud." He steps around the desk to stand behind her, warm hands running up her sides and leaning down to kiss her neck. His hands move up her arms to her shoulders, and he tugs her hair out of the loose bun, letting the dark waves fall down her back. He pushes her hair to one side, continuing to kiss her skin.

She grins, leaning into his touch, then takes a breath before beginning.

"Kimberly sits in the desk chair in front of her computer. The room is empty, and her mind wanders to the exciting rendezvous from the night before."

She looks back at him with a grin and a quick kiss, tasting herself on his mouth, then glances back down.

"Recalling the touch of William's lips on her skin, she shivers, and her hand slides lazily down to stroke her side through the thin material of her flowered dress."

Kimberly glances down at the black dress she wears, but lets her hand slip down, all to aware of how much her actions mirror the few moments before William arrived.

William continues to kiss her neck, hands pressing close through the dress. "I didn't know what you would be wearing," he admits. "Though I did think you'd wear panties." His fingers slide over her ass, tracing the line where her panties would be. "I was looking forward to taking them off you again."

Kimberly shrugs, pressing herself against him, feeling the hardness of his cock against her back. "What can I say? Some guy left with them last night and never gave them back."

"Sounds like a real bastard," William comments, hands sliding the bottom of her dress up so he can caress the skin beneath.

Kimberly nods, her loose hair caressing her skin. "Oh yeah, but he fucked like a champion."

"Did he now?" William asks, fingers sliding between her thighs, stroking her clit with his thumb. "Did he fuck this pussy? Tell me more."

"I didn't know I could come so many times in a row," she tells him, her hand reaching down to rest on top of his, loving the feeling of his hands on her skin. "He just knew how to touch me in all the right places."

William nods, then plucks the folder from her hand, laying it on the desk in front of them and turns her around to face him and then pushes her gently back into the chair. "How did he touch you?" he whispers. "Show me those right places."

Her hand pushes the dress up, revealing her flushed skin, and her other hand grabs her breast, rubbing the nipple gently. "He rubbed my nipples," she says, mimicking the motion as she speaks, "and he kissed my clit."

"Show me," he repeats, cock hardening as he watches her fingers move down to slide along her clit. She can see the outline in his pants, and his voice has roughened.

She strokes the small nub, then drags her finger along the length of herself. "He had these wonderful fingers," she tells him, "and he knew just where to put them." She rubs herself again, short slow bursts that cause her toes to curl.

"And then he put his fingers inside me," she says, her fingers doing the same, disappearing into her pussy, but her thumb stays out and with a slight adjustment of her hand, starts to rub her clit while her fingers move in and out slowly.

"He made me so hot," she says, the motion of her hand increasing in speed and pressure, and her other hand squeezes her nipple hard and she gasps, closing her eyes in her pleasure.

"He made you come," William observes, voice low as his hand brushes against his cock. "Show me now. Show me how you came for him."

"Show me that cock," she says suddenly, eyes opening as she looks at him. "I want to see it again!"

"This cock?" William grins, hands quickly unzipping his pants and tugging himself free from both pants and boxers. He leaves both up on his hips, but strokes himself a few times, giving her an eyeful of his hard cock.

"Yes," she moans, hand moving faster. "I wanted him to fuck me with that cock." She licks her lips, eyes slitted with pleasure. "Will you fuck me with your cock?" she asks, and he strokes himself again, biting his lip as he watches her come, the orgasm shuddering through her.

He gives her a moment to recover, then leans forward to take her face in his hand. "Lovely," he says, then kisses her hard, lips demanding as she shudders in the chair before him, her hands reaching out to grab his cock, her fingers wrapping around his length and squeezing. She pushes him back on the desk, and scoots the chair forward, not letting go of him. He leans back on the desk, very aware of the glass door behind them, across the room, but still totally see-through if anyone were to approach. Kimberly grins up at him.

"No worries," she orders. "Anyone coming in would only see your back, and you'd just be sitting on the desk." She leans down to take his cock in her mouth, but not before adding, "Besides, no one comes in here at night."

William leans back as the warmth of her mouth encloses his cock. She takes him in deep, then slides back up, setting up a slow rhythm designed to break him. He moans, the sound escaping him in a long low rush, and she keeps up her pace, tongue swirling around the sensitive tip each time she pulls up, only to suck hard as she moves back down. Her hand cups his balls, fingers pressing the soft skin hard against him in the same rhythm. She doesn't speed up, knowing that she doesn't want him to come yet, but well aware of what her torturous speed is doing to him.

She remembers how he came the night before, quietly shuddering behind her as they hid from the janitor, and she decides that tonight will be different. She releases his cock from her mouth, replacing it with her hand slowly stroking him up and down, and she looks up at him.

"So, does your story include the couch in the back room?"

He jerks, eyes swiveling back to her as he tries to process what she said. "What back room?" he asks, brain finally understanding what she has said. She gestures with her eyes to the doorway in the middle of the back wall behind the desk. William follows her gaze, but he clearly hasn't realized that the door opens to an employee lounge.

She stands but doesn't release his cock from her grip. She moves, and he slides off the desk to follow. She walks him to the door, his hands holding his pants at his hips, and she puts in the code to open the door. The lock flashes green, and she pushes the handle down, opening the door and pulling him through. She walks him over to the small brown couch that sits against the back wall, then pushes him onto it, releasing his cock as he sits down hard.

"Wait here," she orders, then walks across the room and back out into the public part of the Tutoring Center. She walks to the glass door, makes sure that no one is walking down the hallway toward her, and flips the sign to say CLOSED. She turns off the light so the room goes dark, then navigates by the lights of the computers back to the desk. She collects the blue folder and William's bag, and heads back to the back room, entering the code again to unlock the door. William is sitting where she left him, and he notices the dark room behind her as the door swings shut again.

"Closing early?" he asks.

She nods. "Oh yes. It appears that something has come up that requires my immediate attention."

"What would that be?" he asks, leaning back into the couch cushions, hard cock standing proud from the tumble of his pants.

"I wanted to hear you this time," she tells him, dropping his bag and the blue folder on the table next to the door.

"Hear me?" His eyebrow raises as he looks at her. "What do you mean?"

"I want to hear you come for me," she says. "I don't want you to hold back like you did in the stairwell."

He grins. "There was someone sitting on the stairs," he reminds her. "I hardly dared to breathe too loudly."

She nods. "Exactly. I want to know what sounds you make when you aren't worried about being caught."

He looks around the windowless room, taking in the couch, the table surrounded by a few chairs, and the small black refrigerator pushed into the corner with an ancient microwave sitting on top of it. The microwave is so old that it has a turn dial; for a moment, William can't focus on anything else.

"It would be nice to not have to worry about someone walking in on us," he admits, then glances again at the microwave. "Doesn't that thing give you cancer?"

She chuckles, making her way over to him. "Probably. No one uses it anymore, but no one wants to carry it out of here and throw it away."

He nods, accepting her explanation. The college has lots of old things lingering in odd places, like the extra gym mats under the stairwell last night. He gives the room one more look. "How do you know no one will hear us in here? You can be quite loud."

"I was loud because the stairwell echoes," she says pertly, kneeling before him and taking his cock back into her hands. But then it's her turn to look at the microwave. "That thing is crazy loud, but when you're in the room out there, you can't hear it at all. We think it's because of the bookshelves." She thinks of the bookshelves that line the back wall of the Tutoring Center, filled with textbooks from all of the classes, shelves straining from the weight of all that paper.

William raises an eyebrow, watching as she leans down to lick the tip of his cock. "I thought you said no one used it."

She shrugs, then sucks him hard before releasing him just as abruptly. "Not anymore, I said. But we did a test run." She chuckles. "Like I said, it's dead around here at night—and we used to have two people on shift." She continues to slowly slide her hand up and down his shaft, a teasing rhythm.

"What happened?"

"Budget cuts, mostly. Eventually, we will just close us up at 5 with everyone else, but for now, we follow the library schedule." She sighs, rolling her eyes as she recites: "Open until 8 so last minute students can get tutored."

"Does anyone ever come in at night?"

She shrugs, hands reaching up to unbutton the top few buttons of his shirt, and then she watches him tug it up over his head by grabbing the back of the neck in that magical way that men remove shirts. "Every now and then, but not regularly. And definitely not this time in the semester. Maybe around midterms and always more around finals, like they can just magically understand a semester's worth of work in an afternoon." She shrugs again. "I don't generally mind the empty hours. I find ways to entertain myself."

William smiles, watching her hands on his cock. "I see." She leans down to take him deep into her mouth again and he moans, low and slow. "You are going to leave yourself hanging if you keep doing that," he tells her, and she chuckles, the sound vibrating through his shaft as she releases him. She pauses long enough to unlace his boots and tug them off, then pulls his pants and boxers off. For the first time, William is completely naked. She takes a moment to appreciate the sight.

"I'd hate to leave myself hanging," she admits, but then leans forward to take his cock into her mouth for another few long lazy strokes, "but I do love to suck this cock."

"How would you like to fuck this cock?" he asks, pulling her up.

Kimberly giggles, "I thought you'd never ask." She climbs on to the couch, sliding her dress up as she settles herself on his lap, the warm heat between her thighs sliding around a little until she finds the tip of his cock and presses him against her. She moans, "Oh yes, that's nice," then slides the very tip inside her.

She pauses there, and William grabs her hips under the dress, sliding it up and over her head. Instead of tugging it completely off, though, he leaves it on her arms, and pulls both arms down over his head, trapping her on his lap with her hands wrapped in the dress behind his head. His hands return to the bare skin of her waist then, and he presses her down suddenly, his cock plunging deep inside of her, and she arches her back in pleasure, hands and arms straining against the dress holding her close to him. She moves as if to release herself, but he uses both arms to hold her close against him, setting a brisk rhythm with his hips.

"Oh no," he says into her neck, then uses one hand to pull her face down to his, his other hand still setting the rhythm on her hip, lips claiming hers with a fierce possession. "You are mine now," he tells her, sucking her lip in his excitement. She leans closer into him, body sliding up and down his cock, and he can feel the orgasm building, her pussy tightening around him, and then she cries out, and he smothers the sound with another passionate kiss, and she shudders against him.

"Fuck," she moans after he releases her mouth. "You are so good." She sits back as far as her dress will allow, then glances at him to see if he will release her arms.

"And you," he says, standing up in an athletic display, tugging her arms and the dress over his head, and flipping her so she lays beneath him on the couch, "are the loveliest thing I've ever seen."

He stares down at her for a long moment, one knee on the couch and his other leg standing straight. He reaches forward to push her arms, still tangled in the dress, over her head, and presses them hard into the couch cushions before sliding his hand down her body, caressing her breasts and then sliding down to stroke her pussy again. "So wet for me," he tells her. "I want you to come again for me."

"Yes please," she agrees.

"Greedy girl," he says, then leans down to lick her clit, the motion sending a shudder through her body. "I want to watch you come again."

He licks again, burying his face against her, and then looks up the line of her body to see her face, eyes hooded with desire as she watches him. He reaches a hand up to hold a breast, and then her body is tightening, the orgasm rushing through her. "God yes!" she cries, then jerks away from him.

"Oh no," he insists, tugging her closer and settling a knee on the couch between her legs, leaning down so he can fuck her again. He lays his body on top of hers, hard cock plunging into her in one swift motion, and his other arm presses hard on her upraised arms, pinning her in place. "You wanted this cock?" he asks, hips moving fast and hard now. "You like this cock in your tight pussy?"

"Yes," she moans, body clinging to him, "Yes! Fuck me with your cock!"

He moves faster, harder, and she feels the pleasure rising in him with each stroke. "Come for me!" she screams, "Come in my pussy!" She wraps her legs around his hips, urging him on. "I want to hear you come!"

"Fuck yes!" William yells, burying himself in her in a few frantic strokes, and then he shudders with a wordless shout, body going taut above her. He manages a few more short jerky movements, then collapses on her, heart pounding against her chest so that the beat echoes in her skin. Kimberly lays there for a moment, enjoying the total bliss of complete satisfaction, and then she tries to take a deeper breath and is stopped by the weight on her chest. William seems to return to himself and lifts up on one elbow, relieving the pressure on her chest so she can breathe again, and she takes a deep breath.

"Wow," he mumbles, leaning toward the back of the couch to give her more room. He releases her arms and the dress, and scoots off to the side so he lays next to her on his side, his back pressed against the back of the couch. Kimberly brings her arms down with a groan and shucks off the remains of the dress, tossing it across the room to land on the floor. She reaches out to stroke his face, and then he leans down to kiss her, slow and languorous, enjoying the feel of her mouth without the demands of desire.

"I do hope that was sufficient entertainment," he says later, fingers lazily tracing circles around her nipples.

She smiles slowly, satisfaction and contentment evident in her expression. "Oh yes," she tells him. "I have to close early more often."

"And just think," he adds, "you didn't even get to read my story."

She raises an eyebrow. "Was it anything like this?"

He purses his lips. "Some yes. Some no." He trails a kiss along her neck and down to her nipple. "I want you to read it the next time you're here alone."

"You don't want me to read it to you?" she asks.

He shakes his head. "I did, originally, but it's far more fun to think of you reading it while you're here, thinking of me and all of the things I'm going to do to you."

She smiles up at him, "And will you be doing all of those things to me?"

He leans down to kiss her again, soft this time and burning with promise. "Oh yes. We still have to discuss the matter of your panties."

ENGLISH
MATHEMATICS
PHYSICS
CHEMISTRY
HISTORY
LITERATURE

AbraXus Tasker College Junior Year

Athletics

Ali Whippe

DEDICATION

FOR ALL THE BOYS ON THE TEAM

TABLE OF CONTENTS

1   101

2   105

3   114

4   123

1

$\mathcal{B}$ ree Johnson stands outside the glass door of the Tutoring Center, lips pursed as she contemplates the darkness within. She checks her watch: 6:48pm. She re-reads the posted hours on the door: Mon-Thurs 10am-8pm; Fri-Sat 10am-4pm; Sun Closed.

She leans into the glass, cupping her hands around her eyes to peer in, but she can see nothing beyond the light glow of some computer monitors. The overhead lights are off, and no one moves within.

"Dammit!" she curses. "Isn't it Wednesday?" She looks down at her watch again, tapping the button on the side so it switches from the time to the date.

"Wait—why is it closed?" a voice says from behind her. "I thought they were open until 8 tonight."

"Me too," Bree commiserates, turning to face the newcomer— and all thoughts of studying flee her mind. He is big, like football player big, with broad shoulders and thick legs, a shock of brown hair framing an open, easygoing expression. "Isn't it Wednesday?" she squeaks, trying to ignore the flush of desire that pools in her middle. She has always been a sucker for the boys on the team back home.

"I thought so," he says, scanning the hours as she had done. He steps around her, careful of his size, moving slowly like one who is accustomed to the world being too small for him. He leans in as she had, cupping one hand around his eyes to see through the dark glass, then shrugs. "Maybe Miss Chapman got sick?"

Bree lifts her shoulders in return. "I guess, but she could have put up a note or something." She turns away, thoughts of studying and the test on Friday swamping her brain again. "Fuck," she curses. "I really needed someone to run through flashcards with me."

"Flashcards?" the guy repeats. "You need like a study partner?"

She turns back to look at him, taking in the XTC Stallion t-shirt tight across his chest, the simple black gym shorts ending at his knees, the white tube socks and black Adidas slides. "I don't know," she replies. "What do you know about A&P?"

He cocks his head, "Depends. You mean 'A&P,' the short story by John Updike or A&P like Anatomy and Physiology, the class?"

She stares at him, shock obvious on her face. She didn't expect him to be built like that and actually smart. There is a good chance he is smarter than she is! She took Comp 2 the previous year, so she remembers the short story. "I remember the girls in bathing suits from 'A&P,'" she offers. "How could I forget?"

"Why? You like girls in bathing suits?"

She smirks. "Duh. Who doesn't?" She smiles warmly at him. "But I remember because I had the hottest professor who read it out loud to us in class. He had the best voice," she adds.

The guy nods. "It's a good story, but you're not here to write a paper tonight, are you?"

Bree shakes her head. "No, I have an A&P test on Friday, like the class about the body." She looks down at the floor, suddenly wishing she is wearing something cuter than her pink sweatpants and white tank top, though the black bra showing through is a nice touch she hopes he appreciates.

He nods in understanding, "I took that last semester. It would have been brutal if Coach hadn't made us study constantly. I don't think I'll ever forget about the integumentary system." He raises an eyebrow at her suggestively. "I kept forgetting what it was, and Coach made me run laps until I could remember." He chuckles. "Very long night." He pauses, then adds, "Very effective."

Bree gives him a confused look. "Integu-what?"

"Integumentary," he says again, the word rolling off his tongue. "You know," he says, reaching out to touch her hand. "Skin."

"Oh," she breathes, letting him hold her hand for a long moment. "Right." She stares at him, brain trying to focus on anything, and then she blurts, "What are you here for?"

He shrugs. "I wanted to pick up a review sheet that Vince left for me," he says, "but I guess I can get it tomorrow. Not like I'm going to work on chemistry tonight anyway. I just wanted to have it for later."

"Vince?" she asks. "Is that your friend?"

"One of the guys on the team," he tells her. "He's the wide receiver."

"Is that an innuendo for something?" she asks, hoping he isn't gay. She doesn't think so, but it's always better to ask. She takes in that big body again, hope blooming in her belly. Maybe she can get something out of tonight after all.

He chuckles. "Oh no," he says, flashing her a charming smile. "Vince is as hetero as they come. Me too, though I can admit when a man is handsome as fuck."

Bree smiles back at him, very aware of his hand on hers. "I also enjoy handsome men," she says, an offer in her voice, but then she remembers her test, and other thoughts leave her mind. Her shoulders slump. "What am I going to do about that stupid test? I'm so screwed."

"Well, I could help, if you wanted," he offers.

"Really?" she asks, excitement and something else building in her chest. "With the test or the screwing?" The words spill out, and she blushes.

"Both, if you like," he offers.

"But you hardly know me," she objects. It isn't the first time she hooked up with someone she just met, but she doesn't want him to know that right away.

"No, but I'd like to get to know you." He reaches out his other hand as if to shake. "I'm Josh, cornerback for the XTC Stallions."

Bree nods like she knows what that means. She has spent a fair amount of time listening to football players talk about the sport, but she has spent most of it admiring their bodies, so position names never really matter much. She thinks he is probably a defensive player, judging by his size, and probably does something about guarding the corners of the field. She shakes his offered hand, her other still holding him, "I'm Bree, A&P noob and football fan."

"Tell you what," he suggests, leaning in, "I can help you with those flashcards."

"Really?" she asks, this time her voice skeptical. "I have a feeling we might get distracted. And I really can't fuck this one up."

He nods, face open and sincere, though flirtatious as well. "I solemnly swear I will help you learn those flashcards tonight. Scout's honor." He holds up his fingers like a Boy Scout. "What part are you on?"

"The skeleton," she groans. "I have to label all of the bones."

He nods, lifting up both of her hands, fingers pressing on the tips of hers, "Phalanges," he identifies, then slides his fingers up a little, "Metatarsals." He reaches her palm, gently squeezing the bones there, "Tarsals."

"You do know your anatomy," Bree breathes, turned on and hopeful at the same time.

"You'd be surprised," Josh says, tugging her hand to lead her away from the dark doorway. "Come back to my dorm, and I'll show you all of the bones."

Bree smiles at him. Maybe this actually can work. Nothing says she can't have sex and study tonight. Suddenly, A&P seems a lot more interesting.

2

osh opens the door to his dorm and gestures for Bree to enter. She isn't quite sure what to expect—is he a sloppy guy with clothes everywhere or a tidy guy with everything perfectly in place? She is glad to see that he is somewhere in between. The room is clean enough, but the blanket on the bed against the right wall is rumpled at the foot, the desk covered with several piles of papers. The other desk also has piles, but they seem neater, and the bed only has a plain white sheet on it, no blanket or pillows. There are several pairs of shoes next to the door—a mix of slides and sneakers. Far more shoes than Bree thinks Josh should have if he lives here alone. She glances to her right, seeing the open doorway into a small interior hallway with what looks like a door to the bathroom on the left and another room like this one on the far side.

"You live here alone or with roommates?" she asks, turning to face him as he enters behind her.

"It's a quad," he tells her, "but there's only three of us in here right now. Tony just went home—he broke his leg at the game two weeks ago." He looks at her, tapping his thigh, "The femur, actually."

"I do know that one," she replies with a grin. As she watches, he grabs a sock from the top of the dresser next to the door, and in a smooth motion, hooks it on the outside of the door before shutting it. "Subtle," she tells him with a grin. "Why don't you just lock the door?"

He flips the lock and turns to her. "Because I still have two idiot roommates who don't always take a hint," he admits.

"Do they often walk in on you when you are occupied?"

He nods, "They walk in this way all the time." He gestures at the shoes piled next to the door. "They have their own entrance, but they put an entertainment center in front of it so they can play Madden on a big screen."

"And you don't mind?" she asks, taking the few steps across the room to sit on the empty bed.

He shrugs. "It's a pretty nice TV," he admits, "and I love Madden. Small price to pay to share my doorway."

"Except when you bring a girl back to your room," she observes.

He smiles, walking over and sitting on his bed across from her. "It's not like this happens all the time," he tells her. "Besides, this is an official study session."

"Of course," Bree agrees, setting her bag down on the floor next to her and taking off her flip flops. She tucks her feet up so she sits cross legged. "Totally official."

"So," he says, leaning back and crossing his feet at the ankles, shirt tightening to show off his muscled arms, "let's see those flashcards."

Bree leans down to get them from her bag, moving slowly, deliberately flashing her cleavage as she does so. When she leans back up, his eyes move from her black bra back up to her face and then down to the stack of pink index cards she now holds. She frowns, sexy time on hold as she remembers the test again. "So how do you want to do this?"

He reaches out, long arms easily crossing the space between the beds, and she hands him the cards. "How about we make it a game?" he suggests.

"What kind of game?" she asks, turning her body to face him, wishing he would move closer to her.

"The kind where I ask you a question, and if you get it right, you get a prize, but if you get it wrong, you get a punishment."

"I'm interested," she says, "but what is a prize and what is a punishment?"

"What do you want it to be?" he asks, leaning on his knees so his upper body is closer to hers. She scoots forward on the bed so her legs hang off the edge, her feet nearly touching his. "What would be a prize for you, Bree? What do you want?" His voice has gone low, sexy.

"I want you," she says immediately.

"How do you want me?" he encourages, voice a low thrum that sends shivers up her spine.

Bree looks up at him, eyes tracing from his handsome face down that neck to those gorgeous shoulders. "I want you naked," she says boldly.

"Okay," he agrees," so that's your first prize. Now what about punishment? What do you not want?" he asks.

"I don't want you to murder me since I'm now alone in your room and I hardly know you," she blurts out.

He snorts, leaning back. "I don't plan to do anything of the sort," he promises.

"Just what a murderer would say," she quips.

"Scout's honor," he swears, lifting his three fingers in her direction. "I much prefer you alive. Maybe punishment is the wrong word though..."

Bree frowns at him. "Why don't we just figure it out as we go along?" she suggests.

He smiles in agreement, turning to the flashcards in his hands. "Ready?" Bree nods, and he holds up the card. "Tarsals," he announces.

Bree lifts up her foot, stretching out her shapely leg, and wiggles her toes.

"Nicely done," he says. "I guess that means a prize." He leans down and removes one of his socks.

She smirks at him. "Next."

He flips the card. "Patella."

She points to her kneecap. He tugs off his other sock and turns over the next card. "Ulna."

She lifts her arm and points to the bone on the inside of her lower arm. He nods, stands up, and pulls off his shirt in one smooth motion. Bree gapes at the lines of his muscles, his athlete's body making her mouth water. She reaches out as if to touch him, but he sits back down just out of her reach and picks up the stack of cards. "Clavicle."

Bree reaches up and traces the line of her shoulder, pushing her black bra strap down as she does so along with the strap of her white tank top.

"I don't know," he says. "That's also your humerus."

"Totally counts," she assures him. "Take off your pants."

He smiles, stands up, and slides his shorts off in one smooth motion. He is not wearing anything underneath them, and Bree is rewarded with a large cock level with her face. "I seem to be naked," he observes. "Renegotiation time."

"I'm totally going to suck that cock," she promises him. "I just need to get one more right."

He nods, reaching behind him for the pile of cards, flipping the top one over. "Fibula."

Bree taps the inside of her lower leg and slides off the bed onto her knees, crawling across the small space to take him in her hands, but he steps back and sits down on the bed again. "Oh no," he moans. "That's not right."

Bree sits back on her heels and looks up at him from where she sits on the floor, unable to take her eyes off his cock. "What?"

"Fibula," he repeats, then taps the outer bone of his lower leg. He touches the inner bone, "Tibia."

"So what?" she breathes, sitting up on her knees and reaching for him.

"So that means it's time for a punishment." He stands up, reaching down to grab her hands, and lifts her easily to her feet. "Whatever shall I do with you?" he muses, spinning her around so her back is to him, his cock hard against her back. He holds her arms up over her head with one hand and lets his other slide down her arm and back to rest against her backside. "I think you might need more motivation," he says, whispering in her ear as he half turns her, pressing her side and hip against his chest. He moves his hand in a quick motion and slaps her ass.

"Oh!"

His hand is back again, cupping her ass where he just hit and squeezing. "Too much?" he asks, trailing a soft kiss along her neck.

"Oh no," Bree sighs. "I deserved that." She spins to look at him, keeping one hand up over her head and resting the other against his shoulder. He gently lifts her hand off him.

"Not yet," he tells her, releasing her other hand. "You have to get more right answers."

"You are an awful study partner," she accuses him, blowing out a breath and stepping back. "Fine. Next."

"I am a wonderful study partner," he chuckles, reaching behind him for the stack of cards again. "Maxilla."

She grins, a finger sliding up her body to rest against her upper lip. "I think I deserve a prize," she announces at his nod, and she steps forward again, eager hands reaching out to hold him. His cock is hard and smooth, and she wants more. She reaches up her other hand to touch his face, running a finger along his upper lip. "Maxilla," she repeats, and tugs him down to kiss her. His mouth is warm, lips soft as he opens them, tongue pressing against hers in a gentle rhythm to match the one she uses on his cock.

Josh breaks the kiss after a long moment, his cock hard with a small bead of wetness at the tip. He spins her around and pushes her down on his bed behind them, lifting her easily into place and settling himself on his knees between her legs. "I think you are ready for more intense studying," he tells her, sliding his hands beneath her tank top to stroke the smooth skin of her belly. Bree leans back into his pillow, moaning a little when his fingers find her nipple over her bra. She reaches around to take it off, but he grabs her hand and presses it above her head. "Oh no," he tells her. "Not yet." He traces a finger down between her breasts. "Identify this bone," he whispers.

Bree racks her brain for a moment, and then the word comes to her. "Sternum," she replies, and he smiles at her, pushing her tank top up and freeing her breasts from her bra. He brushes her nipples with his fingers, and pauses right above her, warm breath teasing her skin.

His hand trails along the side of her body, finding the bottom bone of her ribcage. "And this one?"

"12th rib," she answers, and he sucks one nipple, his right hand rubbing the other, his left still pinning her arms over her head.

Bree moans, sensation flooding her. She lifts her legs to wrap around him, trying to pull him closer, but he gently pulls away. "No," he chides, "you still have some studying to do!" He sits back, leaning on his knees, and looks down at her, studying her body, then says, "You're definitely wearing too many clothes for this." He slides the tank top over her head, and unclips her bra with skill that speaks of serious practice. Bree watches him slide her sweat-pants down her hips, delighted to see his eyes light up when he sees her simple white panties.

"Very nice," he observes, tossing her pants behind him to land on the floor in front of the door. He bends down to kiss her nipple again, this time focusing on the right and then the left with the gentle pressure of his mouth. Bree slides her hands down from where he has left them above her head and wraps them around his head, pressing him to her chest.

"Yes," she tells him. "Suck it like that!" He obeys for another long moment, then pulls away, sliding down her body so his face hovers above her belly button.

"You want more?" he asks, trailing a line of kisses down from her lower belly to the top of her panties.

"Oh yes," she moans. "Much more."

His hand moves down to her foot and starts a slow run back up her leg, and he softly sings, "The foot bone's connected to the leg bone... the leg bone's connected to the hip bone...

Bree giggles. "If only it was that easy! I wouldn't need to study anything."

"Let's see..." he says, trailing his hand around her hip. "What's this?"

Bree racks her brain. She knows this one—but she is distracted by his hands on her skin, his face so close to her. "Ilium!" The word bursts from her, and Josh smiles, sliding her panties off and kneeling between her legs. He kisses her gently directly on the clit, warm breath sending pleasure zinging through her, then looks up at her, judging her reaction. His tongue reaches out to press hard against her body just above her clit. "And this?" he breathes, watching her face closely over the hills and valleys of her body.

"Pubis," she moans and is rewarded by his tongue, warm and wet against her skin. His hand moves along her inner thigh, fingers pressing inside her in a slow maddening rhythm to match his tongue.

"You've been so good," he tells her, breath warm on her sensitive skin, fingers continuing to move. "I think you've earned another reward."

"Please," she moans, lifting her hips to his face, and he licks her again, his tongue not wasting any time in finding the perfect spot and staying there, his fingers and mouth bringing her to the edge of an orgasm and right over it in moments. She trembles against him, all thought of bones fleeing her mind until she is entirely made of sensation. "Yes!"

He seems to forget himself then, sliding up her body to place the head of his cock against her. "You want me?" he asks, leaning down to kiss her neck and up to her chin. "You want me inside of you?"

Bree grabs his ass with both hands and pulls him closer, the echoes of the orgasm still radiating in her core, and wraps her legs around his hips. "Fuck me," she orders. "Now!"

Josh obeys, sheathing himself in one swift motion, and Bree shudders against him, hands splayed flat on his ass. "Yes!" she cries. He moves fast for a few strokes, hard and sure, and Bree clutches him hard again as the orgasm sweeps over her. He pauses, letting the moment shatter her, and he shifts, sitting up and lifting her so she sits on his lap, legs wrapped around what Bree notes are more like 12-pack abs. She moves her hands to his shoulders, using him to brace herself as she moves on him, setting the pace to her liking. She is about to come again, enjoying this new position, when he puts both hands on her hips, holding her steady and slides them around and down to cup her ass. "And this?" he asks, moving his head down to kiss her neck and shoulder.

"Uh…" Bree said, focusing on the building need in her center. "My…" She lets the word hang in the air, only needing a few more strokes to get there, and when he moves his hands back to her hips to stop her, she has just reached the edge, and sits still on him, body tightening reflexively as pleasure shoots through her again. After a moment, she looks at him with clear eyes, "What… What were you asking?"

He smirks at her. "Greedy girl!" He stands up, lifting her easily, then spins around and presses her back to the bed. He begins pumping into her hard, responding to the way she moans, the way her body curls around his.

"Yes!" she cries. "More!"

Just as she is about to come again, he pulls out of her completely and pauses. Bree tries to push herself closer, to get that cock back inside of her, but he holds her in place easily. She likes how strong he is, though at the moment, it is a little frustrating. She pouts at him.

"No," he tells her. "Not until you get it all right." His hand slides underneath her ass again, squeezing tight. "What's this called?"

"Ischium," she tells him proudly, the word floating into her mind, and presses forward again. "Now give me that cock."

Josh obliges her. "You definitely earned it!" He lets himself go, pounding into her with furious strokes, her nails digging into his back and her cries muffled against his neck, and he kisses her hard, claiming her mouth, and she comes again, and so does he, and he moves a few more times to enjoy the moment, and pauses, body pressed on top of hers, breathing heavily, hear pounding against her chest.

"Wow," Bree breathes, slowly catching her breath. "We should totally study together more often."

Josh chuckles, then slides to the side so he can rest next to her. "I expect you tomorrow night for chemistry review," he says.

"I'm not very good at chemistry," Bree tells him.

"I don't think we have to worry about chemistry," Josh says, leaning over to give her a long, slow kiss. "Besides, I have flashcards."

3

$\mathscr{B}$ree walks through the sliding doors into the XTC Stallions Sports Facility and takes a moment to marvel at the newness of the building. Most of her classes are in the Science and Humanities buildings, leftovers from the 70s obsession with block construction, but the Sports Facility is brand new and shiny with amenities. Bree reminds herself not to call it the gym, recalling Josh and the twins' faces when she said she'd meet them at the gym for midterm review.

"It's not a gym, Bree," Ryan told her. "It *has* a gym."

"Must be nice," she retorted. "The rest of us little people just have to settle for old showers in the dorms and no windows in the hallways. You guys get all the perks."

"It's not all guys," Bryan commented.

Standing in the lobby, Bree understands what they have been trying to tell her. To her right is a doorway painted with the Stallion logo, a horse in purple and silver. To the left is another door that clearly leads to a pool. Bree can smell the faint aroma of chlorine from where she stands. Maybe after the study session tonight she can get in a swim.

She turns to her right and opens the Stallions door. She is in a big hallway with many doors on both sides. She can see a state-of-the-art gym on one side with fancy weight-lifting machines and high-tech treadmills. On the other side is what she assumes is a locker room, but when she walks inside, she is even more impressed. This is the cleanest locker room she's ever seen, more like the facilities for professional sports teams she's seen on TV than the high school locker rooms Bree has been in. She can hear showers running toward the back right corner of the space, and she can feel the steam in the air, so she assumes practice has finished and Josh and the boys will be ready for her soon.

There are actual lockers lining the wall to the left with two long wooden benches in front of them, and on the right is a wider bench against the wall that turns at the corner and continues along the far wall. In the corner sits the huge mascot costume, the body of the purple and silver stallion sagging back into the corner and the head resting separately on the bench beside it. Along the outside of the shower wall are two large steel bathtubs, one clearly steaming with hot water, and the other filled but not hot. A few large low-to-the-ground massage tables fill the rest of the space along the back wall. There is another hallway in the back corner, and Bree assumes it leads to the practice field behind the building, and probably the coach's office.

Bree wanders over to the hot tub, letting her fingers dip into the water.

"Nice," she mumbles, wishing she could climb in. She assumes the players use it to soothe their aching muscles. "Must be nice."

"It is nice," Bryan says, the tall defenseman walking out of the showers to find her standing by the tub. He wears a white towel wrapped around his hips, the cloth setting off the dark tone of his skin. Bree takes in the muscles of his chest, something she has seen while in Josh's room occasionally, but never so close. He really is a beautiful man.

"What's nice?" Ryan asks, walking in. A mirror image of his brother, the two boys standing next to one another is enough to get Bree's imagination going. She has had a few more "study" sessions with Josh, but she has never played with his roommates. Seeing them bare chested in this light makes her rethink her decisions this semester.

"The tub," Bryan tells him.

'You should get in," a third voice joins them, Josh walking in with a towel as well.

Bree gives them a skeptical look. "Right now? But there's people in here."

Josh shrugs. "It's just us." He looks at the twins. "We had to do a few more drills before Coach was satisfied tonight."

Something in the way he says it makes Bree wonder what Coach Smith considers satisfaction, but the thought flees as she stares at the three beautifully sculpted bodies before her. "Damn." The word escapes her before she can help it, and then she continues boldly. "I don't need my study guide," she admits. "I can just label the muscles on all of you!"

Josh grins, he and the twins exchange a look, and he raises an eyebrow at her. "You up for some rewards tonight?"

Bree meets his gaze fully. "What kind of rewards?"

"That depends on how well you can identify the muscles," he replies, glancing at the twins. "You guys in?"

"That depends on Bree," Bryan says, giving her a look that melts her stomach. "You want us to get in?"

She smiles invitingly, looking from Bryan to Ryan and back again, imagination running wild. The twins are beautiful men, and the idea of sex with all three of the players has her instantly wet. "Three is always better than one," she comments. She glances behind her at the still steaming tub. "What did you have in mind?"

Josh gestures at it. "You should get in," he tells her again.

"What if someone comes in?" she asks, looking around at the empty room. The sound of the showers has stopped, and she can't hear anyone else moving around.

Ryan shakes his head. "No one is coming in here. Everyone is at House of Beer for 2-for-1 Thursdays." Bryan nods his agreement. "We would have joined them, but I think this is more important."

"Thanks, Bryan," Bree says sweetly. "I'm glad you find my academic success so important."

"Anything for a lovely lady." He grins, then moves closer, towel swishing along his hips. "After all," he brags, "you may need someone to model certain muscles for you." He runs a hand down his glorious abs, highlighting that line that runs down to a V beneath the towel. "You can see I am well equipped for the job."

Bree swallows hard, wanting to touch him, to see just how well-equipped he is. He is so close to her now. She looks at Josh, wondering if he will mind, but he smiles at her and nods encouragingly. "Big words," she says, reaching out to touch the hard mass of his abs. "But are you a big man to match?"

Bryan's face is smug as he stands there, letting her run her hands up and down his smooth skin. "I think you will find me up to the job," he promises.

Bree's hands wander lower, finding the edge of the towel, ready to tug it loose, but she looks around first. "What about your coach?" she asks.

"Coach won't come in here," Ryan says, stepping forward to stand next to his brother. "We're all alone."

Bree looks behind them to Josh, who seems to read her mind and walks up on Bryan's other side. She looks at the beautifully sculpted male bodies around her and grins broadly. "So," she says, "how do we begin?"

"How about we start with some muscle identification?" Josh suggests, gently taking her hand and placing it on the outside of his upper arm.

"Bicep," Bree tells him, and Josh nods, lifting her hand away and passing it to Bryan, who places it on his side, just above the towel.

"Abdominal external oblique," Bree says proudly. She is a fan of hips, so she knows that one.

Bryan grins at her. "You seem thoroughly familiar with those," he comments, taking her hand and passing it to his brother.

Ryan drags her hand along his side, then settles it on his belly button. "Rectus abdominis," she whispers. "Guys, I know all these. Abs are my favorite thing."

"Your favorite?" Ryan asks, then gently pushes her hand down over the towel to press against the sizable bulge there. "Really?"

Bree moves her hand down and quickly slips beneath the towel, reaching up to grasp Ryan's huge hard cock. "I'm also a fan of other parts," she says, slowly stroking him.

"Hey now," Bryan says. "My brother and I do everything together." He reaches for her other hand, pressing it to his own bulge, and she snakes her hand beneath his towel, gripping his matching cock and slowly stroking both of them in tandem. After a moment, she glances at Josh on her left.

"What about you?" she asks. "My hands seem to be full."

Josh reaches out to wrap his hands around her waist and lowers her gently to her knees. "I think I can find a place to fit in," he says, lifting his towel up and presenting his own erect cock at the level of her mouth.

"Always room for one more," she agrees, then takes him in her mouth, not breaking the pace of her strokes on the twins' cocks. She sucks for a long moment, and then Josh gently pulls back, not wanting to come too quickly.

"I think you've earned a reward," Ryan says.

"Let us pleasure you," Bryan echoes, and both guys lift her off her knees. Ryan tugs off her tank top as Bryan slides her sweatpants off, revealing her lacy blue bra and matching thong.

"Lovely," Josh breathes. He steps behind her, totally naked, and lifts her easily. Bryan and Ryan each take one of her feet and begin rubbing them with sure hands. Bree can feel Josh's hard cock pressing against her ass, but he holds her steady, not moving at all, letting her focus on the twins' movement instead. Slowly, they move from her feet to her calves and then to her thighs.

They move to stand on opposite sides of her legs, both sliding practiced fingers down her belly and over her thong, now wet with her excitement. "Lift her up," Ryan tells Josh, who obliges, easily hefting her to shoulder height. Bryan steps between her legs, placing one thigh on each shoulder, and moves close, burying his face between her legs. He slides her thong aside easily, tongue swiping across her sensitive skin in one long, luscious motion. Bree shudders against him. Bryan continues to lick her clit as he moves one hand up to slide gently inside her, moving slowly in and out. Bree is about to cry out, but then Ryan is next to her face, and he reaches down to kiss her, one hand tangling in her hair, and the other squeezing a nipple. Ryan's tongue is no less skilled than his brother's, and the two move in tandem. Bree puts one hand against the side of Ryan's face, holding him close to her, and lets the other wander above her head, finding Josh's face. Josh takes her fingers into his mouth, sucking eagerly.

Bree loses herself in the moment, the streaks of pleasure from between her legs, the joy of Ryan's tongue in her mouth, the feeling of weightlessness as Josh holds her aloft, and the orgasm floods her. She shakes against Bryan's face, not aware of much until she feels strong hands sliding her thong down her legs, and more hands unclipping her bra.

Then she is being lowered into warm water, the steaming heat soothing her muscles, and she sinks into pleasure. A hand finds her skin, sliding down her belly to rub her clit in slow generous circles, and she shudders against it again, the pleasure slow and sweet.

After a moment, she opens her eyes and smiles at the three naked men surrounding the tub. Bryan is to her right, so she sits up in the tub, reaches out for his cock and tugs him toward her mouth. He is big, but she can manage his length for short bursts. She sucks for a long time, then releases him, turning to face the others. She kneels at the end of the tub, gesturing for them to stand in front of her and one on each side.

Ryan takes his place at the head of the tub, the only one who she has not sucked yet, and Bryan and Josh stand on either side. She takes both cocks in her hands, slowly stroking them, and leans forward to take Ryan in her mouth. There is a long moment of sucking and stroking, and then Ryan pulls out of her grasp, visibly calming himself.

She leans back, biting her lip and looking around at all three of them. "I'm going to need some of these cocks inside of me," she announces. "Who's first?"

"Oh no," Josh says, gently removing her hand from his cock. "You have to study, remember?" He gestures at the line of muscle that forms a V shape down to his cock. "What's this called?"

"Magical?" Bree asks, leaning forward to trace the line with her tongue. Bryan takes the opportunity to swat her butt. She yelps, sinking back down into the warm water.

"You're magical," Bryan says. "What's it called?"

Bree racks her memory. "Pec-something?" she tries, looking sheepish.

"Nope," Ryan says, leaning down and scoops her out of the tub with one quick motion. She sinks dripping against his chest for a glorious moment, but he moves swiftly across the space. Bree realizes what he is going to do about a second before he drops her into the other tub of water, which Bree notes with a shriek, is ice cold. She splutters, standing up immediately, and jumping out of it. She stands there shivering, watching all three naked men approach. Her eyes move from cock to cock to cock, and she licks her lips.

"I think she wants us, boys," Josh comments.

"But she got it wrong," Bryan says.

"She needs to earn another reward," Ryan echoes.

She looks at the line in question on all three men. "I don't know what it's called," she admits. "But I love it so much!"

"It's called the Adonis Belt," Ryan tells her.

"Or Apollo's Belt," Bryan adds.

"Although your teacher would probably label it as an iliac furrow," Josh supplies helpfully. "And it's not technically a muscle. It's a ligament."

"Cheaters!" Bree accuses. "Ligaments aren't on the midterm."

"I think ligaments might come up tonight," Ryan says, idly stroking himself as he looks at her glistening naked body.

"That's not all that will come up," Bree says, and crooks her finger at Ryan. "Come here, Big Boy. I need to feel that cock inside me."

Ryan steps over to her and lifts her up. She wraps her legs around his waist, gripping his shoulders as she settles herself on his cock. "Yes!" she moans, sinking onto him, his length filling her. He bounces her up and down a few times, holding her easily, his body stroking her clit with each motion, and she comes again, pressing her breasts to his chest as she gasps his name. When she opens her eyes again, he looks down at her in his arms.

"You want more?"

"Oh yes," she says, and then she feels Bryan settling himself against her back.

"How much more?" he whispers against her neck, the tip of his cock pressing against her ass.

"A lot more," she tells them, "but I need more action first."

"Of course," Bryan agrees, lifting her off of his brother, and sets her feet gently on the ground. "How about something more traditional then?" He gestures to the low massage table in the back of the room, and the four of them walk over to it.

"Where do you want me?" Bree asks, crawling on to the leather-covered table on her hands and knees. The padded top barely sinks beneath her weight, the table built to hold two people side-by-side.

"Right there will do," Bryan says, moving up behind her, hard cock sliding inside of her with ease. Bree gasps, and then Ryan kneels in front of her, his cock wet with her juices in front of her mouth. She reaches for it eagerly, taking him deep in her mouth as Bryan begins to fuck her harder from behind.

Josh climbs up on the bed next to her, and just as she is about to come again, he runs his hands down her back and across her ass, one finger circling her asshole and slipping inside. She grunts at the unexpected sensation, and redoubles her efforts, pumping hard against Bryan and sucking Ryan. Another wave of pleasure builds up from her center, and then Josh has two fingers inside of her ass, and she groans her orgasm, body bucking wildly.

Bryan grabs her hips and holds her steady, clearly on the edge himself, but he pulls out. He turns around, sitting on the edge of the table with his feet resting firmly on the floor in front of him, the low table making his thighs angle up to his knees. He tugs Bree close. "Climb aboard," he tells her, and she does, sliding down the incline of his legs and lifting herself on his cock again. She presses her feet into the top of the table, finally gaining the leverage she seeks, and starts to move again, but Bryan shakes his head, hands pressed to both of her hips to hold her steady. "Not yet," he says, standing up and turning to stand next to the table. Bree wraps her legs around his waist, enjoying the fullness of his cock inside of her, eager to see what comes next. Ryan stands up.

"You want more?" Bryan asks her again.

Bree nods, excitement filling her with anticipated pleasure. Ryan moves to stand facing his brother, and Bree feels Ryan's cock pressing against her ass. He slides closer as his brother pushes her backwards, and Bree is slowly filled with both cocks. The twins move slowly in tandem, the motion filling Bree with exquisite sensation.

"Fuck yes!" she cries, moving a little faster, letting herself take them both completely, pleasure scorching her entire body.

"Bree!" Bryan's commanding voice makes her look up at him, and he tilts his head to the side, where Bree realizes Josh has climbed up on the table and is now standing on it, his hard cock about level with her face. "Suck him!"

Bree obeys, relishing in the fullness of her body, the competing sensations building as the boys take her to another level. Bree comes just as Josh explodes, cum filling her mouth and running down her chin, and then the twins roar their own pleasure, and they all stand there for a long moment, lost in pure pleasure.

Slowly, Bree comes back to herself, letting Josh's cock slip out of her mouth. Ryan's cock slides out of her ass, and Bryan lifts her off him and sets her gently on the edge of the table. All three guys collapse on the table around her, everyone breathing hard.

"Well," Bree says, after a long moment where she catches her breath. "That gives a whole new meaning to cramming."

4

"I did so well on my midterm," Bree tells Josh. "I was hoping we could do something similar for finals."

Josh smiles at her as they walk across campus to the Stallions Sports Facility. "Definitely," Josh agrees, looking over his shoulder to where Ryan and Bryan walk behind them. "Don't you worry. We have something special planned."

"Oh?" Bree asks. "Like what?"

"If we told you, it wouldn't be a surprise," Ryan says.

"I hope you like it," Bryan adds, smiling shyly at her.

Bree returns the smile. "I'm sure I will." She grabs Josh's hand as they walk, addressing all three of them. "You guys were a huge help last time. I have an A in A&P right now."

"Great," Josh says. "And tonight, we're going to help you keep it."

They approach the sliding glass doors and walk inside, the cool air-conditioned air hitting them with a blast. Bree follows Josh into the locker room, sitting down on one of the benches in front of the lockers. She has been to their training area many times since studying for midterms, so she is comfortable enough. She's met some of the guys on the rest of the team, so when they walk out from the showers to reach for their lockers, she greets them. None of them seem to mind a girl in the locker room; in fact, they seem to relish strutting around in their towels, flashing her whenever they get the chance.

Bree watches Aaron, the blonde quarterback, as he approaches, taking a moment to appreciate the sculpted muscles of his chest. To her disappointment, he isn't wearing a towel, just gym shorts, but his hair is a little wet, like he just came in from outside.

"Hey Aaron," she says. "How was practice?"

He shrugs, flashing her that perfect smile complete with dimples. "Practice was fine." He looks at Josh. "But I'm looking forward to the afterparty."

Bree raises an eyebrow. "What afterparty? I'm just here to study for finals."

He nods. "I know. I thought we'd get some of the guys to help out, make sure you really know everything you need to." He bites his lip.

Bree cocks her head at him, mind cycling through all manner of fantasies. "What did you have in mind?" she asks the quarterback, hoping he says what she's thinking. Sex with the team is a Bucket List item.

"Well," he says, gesturing at Ryan and Bryan sitting on either side of her, with Josh moving off to her right, "you already know how helpful these guys can be." He looks over his shoulder to the hallway leading out to the practice field. "You know," he suggests, "we could always add more players to the game." He pauses, then adds, "To assist in the … study session."

Bree bites her lip and considers the logistics. "Like how many more?"

Aaron smiles wide. "You already know these three, but how about Vince, Jason, and Corey?" As he says their names, three men walk into the room.

"Vince is our wide receiver," Aaron introduces, gesturing to a tall dark-skinned bald man with a beautiful face. Bree nods at him. She's had a few brief conversations with Vince while he and Josh study for chemistry. The thought of seeing him up close and personal is thrilling.

"Jason is our tight end," Aaron continues, pointing to a lean red-head with a shock of freckles across his pale face. Vince reaches over and smacks Jason on the ass.

"Tightest end in town," Vince says with a laugh.

"You know it," Jason tells him, turning so Bree can see the ass in question. It is a glorious ass, covered as it is in his gym shorts, and Bree nods. She wouldn't mind squeezing some of that ass.

"And you know Corey, our safety," Aaron finishes, nodding at the lean, caramel-skinned man standing on the end. Bree nods at him; she and Corey both had English together last semester.

"Hmm," Bree says, looking at the newcomers in turn. "It depends. How are you guys with body systems?"

"Solid," Vince offers, gesturing at his gorgeous abs. "My body is a perfect system."

"Apparently, I'm the ass man," Jason offers, "but this ass remembers enough to get by."

"I think you know I'm a team player," Corey reminds her. "We will get the job done."

Bree takes in the seven men in the room with her. She smirks. "Anyone else?" She looks around, noting the Billy the Bronco costume leaning in the corner, the purple and silver stallion mascot looking like it decided to take a break and sit down. Bree has the weird feeling that it is watching her, but she shrugs it off. There are enough eyes on her at the moment.

"Well..." Aaron begins.

Bree cocks her head. "What? Is there someone else you had in mind?"

He shrugs. "Phillipe is still outside practicing his kicks."

Bree pictures the beautiful kicker from Colombia, his dark hair, his bright eyes, his long limbs. She nods at Aaron, deciding to swing for the fences. "Sure." She's always wondered what it would be like to taste that mouth.

Aaron nods and Jason takes off, heading out to the back field. When he returns a few moments later with a sweaty but still gorgeous Phillipe, Bree stares at them all in turn: her team.

"So," Aaron says in the silence, "What do you think?"

"I think we should start with some ground rules," Josh offers, winking at her. "Bree is highly motivated by rewards and punishments." He looks at her. "I assume you have more flashcards?"

Bree nods, reaching down for her nearly forgotten bag and pulls out the worn stack of 3x5 cards. She holds them out, not sure who will be in charge of them. Aaron nods his head at the twins, and Ryan reaches out to grab them. "We'll switch off," he tells his brother.

"Let's see," Aaron says. "I think we should start with something easy." He looks at Ryan, who flips the top card and scans it, then shoves it into the middle of the stack and flips to the next one. He seems more pleased with this option.

"Forms the external body covering and protects deeper tissues from injury," he reads. "Contains cutaneous receptors and sweat glands."

Everyone looks at Bree, but she smirks at Josh, who winks at her. She remembers his touch on her skin as he whispered to her. "The integumentary system," she declares proudly.

Aaron nods. "A reward then. What would the lady prefer?"

Bree smiles broadly, a slow rush building in her lower belly. "Yes." She gives them all another once over, some of them still sweaty from practice. "And I think we should definitely start with a shower."

Aaron grins. "Good call." Bree lets the quarterback reach down, grab her slightly sweaty hand from her lap, and pull her gently to her feet. He leads her to the back right corner of the large room, the guys surrounding her in a circle as they walk by the massage tables and pass the two tubs—one filled with steaming water and the other with water Bree knows is icy cold. He pauses outside the open shower area, then slides his hands down to wrap around her waist. He leans down slowly, an offer, and when Bree turns her face up to his, he kisses her, mouth warm and lips soft against hers.

Hands run up her sides and a body presses against her back, a mouth kissing the back of her neck, and Bree recognizes Josh. His hands move slowly around to her front and slip down inside her sweatpants to press on her clit the way he knows she likes. She moans into Aaron's mouth, her hands reaching out and finding hard muscle. Aaron releases her mouth just as Josh's fingers begin to move in a slow sweet rhythm against her, and she leans back against him. Her hands abandon Aaron and reach out to her sides, each encountering smooth skin over hard muscle—Corey and Vince on either side of her.

They respond by sliding the straps of her tank top down her arms, taking their time, reaching under each breast to lift it out of the cami. Bree is glad that she chose not to wear a bra tonight as the straps clear her hand. Together, they push the rest of the tank top down around her stomach, freeing her breasts completely. Hands cup her, fingers gently squeezing her nipples, and combined with Josh's constant rhythm between her legs, Bree comes suddenly, falling back into the cornerback.

He catches her easily, and Aaron releases her mouth, stepping back. Ryan and Bryan step forward and lift each of her legs, letting Corey and Vince slide both her sweatpants and her tank top down, leaving her naked. She shivers, and then she is being carried into the shower where the water is already pouring down from six showerheads, the three stalls on each side divided by a low half wall that juts out about two feet. The center of the shower is open, but still has three rain showerheads that pour water in a flow almost hard enough to massage muscles.

Corey and Vince stand on either side of her as she tilts her head back, letting the flow of the water soak her hair and rinse her face.

"I think it's time for another question," Aaron announces.

"Supports and protects the body's organs and provides the framework for muscles," Bryan reads quickly.

"Skeletal system," Bree tells them proudly, hands sliding from her hair down her body and settling on her hips. She pulls her face out of the stream and looks at them. She meets Jason's eyes and jerks her head at him to stand in front of her. The redhead obliges, sliding his shorts off in an instant and moving into the shower. Bree is pleased to see he has a long, lovely cock standing proudly in a thatch of red hair. She reaches for him, grabbing that cock first, and tugs him closer to her, letting the water flatten his hair to his head. She leans into the flow, hand slowly stroking his cock, and kisses him. Her other hand reaches out to the side, and then Corey's hands are touching hers. She drags his hand to her breast and leaves it there. Vince is quick to get the message, both leaning in to cup her full breasts. She is close to Jason, kissing him, but then she pulls away, and in the moment there is space between her and Jason, Corey and Vince lean in and begin to suck her nipples.

Bree moans, but doesn't lose her grip on Jason's cock, continuing to stroke him. A body moves behind her, and gentle hands caress her sides, and someone is kissing her neck. A hard cock presses against her ass. She turns to find Phillipe and kisses him, head turned to the left, while Corey and Vince continue to suck her nipples. Phillipe is an amazing kisser, and Bree loses herself in the feeling, barely noticing when Corey and Vince seem to shift a little. She does notice when Jason's cock moves out of reach of her hand, and he grabs her hand and moves it off to her right, where she can continue to stroke him where he stands between Vince and Phillipe. Her left hand is suddenly touching another hard cock, and she opens her eyes for a second to find Josh on her left. She grabs the cock and begins stroking in rhythm with Jason and returns to kissing Phillipe.

New hands are suddenly on both of her hips, tugging her forward slightly, and a warm mouth sucks her clit, tongue licking her gently and sucking hard again. She moans, legs going weak at the spike of sensation, and the men support her weight easily. Her nipples contract, pleasure spiraling up from her middle, and she comes hard against the mouth. Through the haze of her delight, she looks down her body to see the blonde hair of Aaron's head between her legs. He looks up at her and winks, then sucks hard again, this time sliding two fingers inside of her. Bree bucks wildly against him, coming again, and she goes boneless for a moment.

Phillipe stops kissing her, and hands hold her steady, but Aaron's mouth leaves her sensitive skin for a moment, giving her a break. Then hands are rubbing shampoo into her hair, and others hands are sliding soap along her skin, and she stands there, regaining the solidity in her legs, letting the men wash her like a queen.

Athletics

When she is completely rinsed, Aaron stands up and says, "I think it's time for another question."

Ryan and Bryan are standing just outside the shower, watching the festivities but not joining in, though each has his cock out and is slowly stroking it. Bree smiles at each in turn, knowing she will have her way with them too, in time.

Ryan lets go of his cock and reaches for the stack of cards resting on the ledge behind him. He flips to the next one, grins, and reads, "Houses white blood cells involved in immunity."

Bree sighs, reveling in the loose feel of her body under the warm water. "I feel pretty immune right now," she moans.

"What's the system?" Bryan asks. "Name it."

"I know it," Bree stalls, trying to get her brain to focus.

"Then tell us," Aaron says, giving her ass a quick swat.

Bree squeaks. "It's the…" Her voice trails off, her brain spinning.

Aaron reaches behind him and shuts off the water, and Bree is standing there, naked and dripping. "I think it might be time for a punishment, boys."

Bree giggles. "I think my punishment should definitely be a cock in the mouth," she suggests, sinking to her knees.

"That's a reward, Bree," Josh says. "You know the rules."

Bree frowns, then thinks again. "Immunity…" Hands reach out to caress her shoulders gently, sliding on her wet skin from the outside of her upper arm and back up to the sides of her neck. "Think, my beauty," Phillipe croons behind her, and the answer hits her. "Lymphatic system!"

"Nice," Aaron tells her. "Now you get a reward." He looks around. "Who would you like?"

Bree scans the eager faces and turns to look at Phillipe behind her. "I think I'll start here," she says, and leans forward to take his cock into her mouth. She takes two slow pulls, then gestures with each hand. Corey and Vince step up immediately, and she is rewarded with a cock in each hand. Aaron kneels behind her, his cock pressing into her back, and he leans down to kiss her neck. She opens her eyes to glance to her right, meeting Josh's eyes as she sucks Phillipe's cock. She turns her head, locking eyes with Jason next, and when she finally turns her gaze up to watch Phillipe's face, the kicker lets loose with a long stream of Spanish before exploding in her mouth. Bree giggles, lets go of Vince and Corey, and stands up, kissing Phillipe hard, cum rolling down her chin. Aaron groans, and then he is standing up behind her, hard cock pressed against her entrance.

"You want this cock?" he asks, and Bree releases Phillipe's mouth long enough to say yes, pushing back against him, eager to feel him inside of her. He slides inside easily, filling her, and she groans, finding Phillipe's mouth again. Her hands reach out to either side, and Corey and Vince are where she left them. She strokes them both as Aaron pumps into her, and soon she is shuddering her release, moaning into Phillipe's mouth as she sinks against him.

Aaron leans back, tugging her backwards, and then he is sitting on the floor, and she is on top of him, her back to his chest. He lifts her gently, letting her slide up and down a few times as he adjusts her legs to spread them wide on either side of his own. Bree moves her feet, attempting to shift into reverse cowgirl position, but he holds her steady. "Oh no," he tells her, trailing kisses along her neck. "Stay like that."

Jason moves between her legs, and Bree reaches out for that long cock, but he leans down instead, face between her thighs, his tongue quick and adept, and soon Bree is coming again, hands pressed against the back of his head. Her heart is still pounding when Aaron gently lifts her off his cock, and then puts his cock against her asshole.

"You ready for this?" he asks.

"Maybe," she replies, "but I want Jason in my ass." She turns around to face him, pressing against his chest until he lays down on the shower floor. She climbs on, relishing the feel of him inside of her again and leans forward. "Josh," she says, gesturing toward him. "Bring me that cock." The cornerback obliges, standing in front of her, a foot on either side of Aaron's head.

Jason scoots in behind her, hands pressing against her ass. Corey and Vince move to either side, lifting her up and down in a gentle rhythm as Jason slides first one and then two fingers into her ass. "Oh yes!" she moans, leaning forward to take Josh into her mouth. She comes hard, the orgasm shaking her, and while she is still recovering, Jason replaces his fingers with his cock, and the thin length slips inside of her. She grunts, and then Bree is aware of nothing but pleasure as both cocks move inside of her. Hands cup her breast, another hand slides down to press against her clit and begins to rub. The sensations quickly overwhelm her, and as she clenches in her orgasm, she feels Aaron let go inside of him. A moment later Jason is also cumming. Josh is the last to let go, and Bree leans back without thinking, cum running down her chin. Vince and Corey lift her away, and someone turns on the shower again.

Hands rub her down, soaping her slowly and gently, and Bree isn't paying attention to who is attached to what anymore. A mouth finds her clit in the warm water, and she sags backwards into another body, who cups her under the arms to hold her upright.

"More?" a voice says, and Bree nods, then finds her voice.

"Yes," she tells them. "I'm not done yet. More."

The shower turns off, and hands carry her out, a soft towel rubbing against her skin. She is laid down somewhere, and Bree opens her eyes to recognize the massage table. Her team surrounds her, and she smiles at them all.

"What now?" Aaron asks.

Bree considers. She looks at Corey and Vince in turn. "I feel like you guys deserve some one-on-one time," she says, crawling up on her hands and knees between them.

Corey takes the hint, scooting up behind her and resting the tip of his cock against her opening. Vince moves to kneel in front of her, cock even with her mouth. She sucks in at the same moment she presses back against Corey, the cock sliding inside of her, ultra-sensitive skin singing in response to the stimulation. "God," she moans against Vince's cock, moving back and forth in a gentle, mind-blowing rhythm. She abandons the cock in her mouth, grabbing him with her hand instead focusing on Corey and that glorious orgasm building again inside of her. "Fuck!" she yells, squeezing

Vince's cock and pressing hard against Corey. "Fuck me!" And then Corey is pounding her, gentleness forgotten, sensitive skin forgotten, and Bree comes again, a scream tearing from her throat. Corey comes hard against her, and she lays there for a moment to collect herself, Vince's cock forgotten in her head.

After a long moment, she looks up at him. "Oh no!" She takes a deep breath. "Come on, Vince," she says. "Your turn."

Vince flips her onto her back, and tugs her toward him, sheathing himself to the core in one motion, setting a fast rhythm as if he knows she doesn't have much left in her. She wraps her legs around his hips, hands gripping his ass, urging him on with grunts and moans. She comes again when he does, and they lay together, sticky with sweat and pleasure. Vince gets up after a moment and falls beside her. Bree lays on her back, breathing hard. Gentle hands stroke her skin, but only to touch, not to come. Her body relaxes, coming down from the intense pleasure, and after a moment, she opens her eyes and leans up on her elbows.

She looks at where the twins are sitting on the edge of the table. "I believe it's your turn," she says. "You definitely deserve something for being such good study partners."

"Speaking of studying," Aaron offers, "I think it's time for another question."

Bree sighs, but leans back. "Hit me," she tells them, trying to get her brain back in study mode.

Bryan stands up to retrieve the cards from where he left them on the edge of the shower. Walking back, he reads the top one, "Pumps blood to deliver nutrients to major organs."

Bree snickers. "Cardiovascular system. I certainly worked mine out tonight."

The twins nod in unison and move closer to her. Bryan grabs her legs and drags her down to the edge of the table. Her legs bend at the knees and her feet land flat on the floor. Bree is short, and the table is very low.

"Wait," Aaron says. There is a low clicking sound, and Bree feels the bed being raised beneath her. Aaron raises it until her feet dangle, and Bryan tugs her the rest of the way to the edge, standing between her legs with his cock pressed against her. Ryan climbs up on her right and kneels next to her. He gives her a quizzical look, head cocked.

"What?" Bree asks.

"Can I fuck those perfect titties?" he asks.

Bree looks down at her chest. "Sure," she says. "Get over here with that huge cock."

Ryan climbs on top of her, sitting on her stomach and sliding his cock between the valley of her breasts. Bree presses them together around him, and Ryan sighs with pleasure. As Ryan begins to move, Bryan slides gently inside her, moving slowly against her battered skin, hands gripping her hips.

Bree closes her eyes again, losing herself in the moment, aware of the eyes of the team on her. She opens her eyes and looks at each of them in turn. "Come on me," she offers. Aaron and Phillipe start to move, but the sound of a voice makes everyone freeze in place.

"And what is happening here?" a lush female voice demands. "I don't recall giving anyone permission to come all over anyone."

Bree turns to stare at the newcomer, a small red-haired woman wearing a white tank top with the Stallions logo and a short purple pleated skirt.

"Coach!" Aaron says. "We didn't think you were still here!"

"Clearly," Coach Smith says, giving the twins a glare. "Did I say you could stop?"

Bryan resumes his motion and Ryan slowly grinds into Bree's breasts while Bree stares at the coach incredulously. "Umm," she stammers. "They are helping me study?"

Coach Smith nods. "I see. And how is it going?"

Bree grins stupidly. "Amazingly," she admits, Bryan's cock hitting that perfect stride inside of her, a low glow building in her belly again, even with the Coach watching. "They are wonderful partners."

"Tell me something I don't know," Coach Smith says. "But how are you?" She gives Bree a long look. "Are you worthy of my boys?"

Bree looks around at the satisfied faces around her. "I think I'm doing just fine," she declares, hooking her legs around Bryan's hips and urging him faster, meeting the coach's eyes and he moves faster in her, hands pressing hard on her breasts as Ryan rocks back and forth, his cock slipping against her skin.

"Let's see," Coach Smith declares, and then she is climbing onto the table, putting one leg on either side of Bree's head, and she squats right on Bree's face, bringing her bare pussy to Bree's open mouth. Bree is so shocked that for a moment she can do nothing, but her hands reach up automatically to cup Coach's perfect ass beneath the skirt, and then she is moving her mouth, marveling at the taste of pussy against her lips, her tongue slipping out to find her clit. The woman bounces on Bree's face, and Bree licks again, her tongue finding a hard bump and sucking it into her mouth.

"Oh yes!" Coach Smith yells. "You are good!" She rocks her hips against Bree's face, and Bree sucks some more, the fingers of one hand sliding a little so she can slide a finger inside Coach's pussy.

"Fuck those titties, Ryan," Coach barks. "I want to see cum everywhere." There is a sound like kissing, and Bree wonders if Coach is kissing Ryan, but then Coach commands, "Fuck that pussy like you mean it, Bryan!"

Bryan obeys, pumping into Bree, and she clutches him with her legs, the orgasm spiraling up hard and fast. "And you," Coach Smith orders, "suck my pussy! I want to come all over that lovely face!" Bree shoves her fingers inside Coach's pussy the way she likes in her own pleasure, mouth sucking hard on her clit, and then the wave hits her and she is shuddering against Bryan as he cums, Ryan's cum floods over her breasts, and Coach Smith trembles against her face with a cry. More warmth hits Bree's skin from other angles, hot liquid running down her skin.

Coach Smith leaps off Bree's face in a display of casual athleticism, and stands there, taking them all in. Ryan and Bryan are breathing hard. Bree's heart is still pounding. The team is kneeling around them on the table, dicks still in their hands.

Athletics

"I hope my boys did you proud tonight," Coach announces. "And good luck on that final exam." She turns and walks out of the room, disappearing down the hallway. A heavy door shuts behind her.

Bree lays there on the table, still catching her breath and licking her lips, the taste of Coach still in her mouth. Ryan leans forward and kisses her slowly, sensually. He releases her, and climbs off her stomach, and Bryan leans down to kiss her as well. He pulls back after a moment, slipping out of her, and then Phillipe is leaning down to kiss her too, followed by slow kisses from Corey, Vince, Jason, and Aaron. Josh waits until the end, then settles in next to her head and kisses her long and passionately.

Bree sits up slowly, body languid and sticky with spent pleasure.

"So," Aaron asks her, "you think you're ready for that final now?"

Bree smiles at him. "Best. Studygroup. Ever.

Extra
CREDIT

Ali Whippe

DEDICATION

FOR EVERY "HOT FOR TEACHER" FANTASY

TABLE OF CONTENTS

1	....	141
2	....	151
3	....	154
4	....	159
5	....	164
6	....	168

1

*J*ustin Cooper looks from his phone to his gym teacher and back again.

"Midterm grades are posted online," Coach Smith says, "and I'll be in my office if anyone has any questions. Otherwise, you're done for the day! Go home." She pauses, then adds, "Don't forget to support the Stallions at the game Friday night." Most of the class stands immediately, grabbing bags and checking phones as they wander out of the room.

Justin stares at the grade on his phone, face heating as he takes in what it says. *C*, he thinks frantically. *I cannot have a C. My GPA cannot take a C, especially for something as stupid as gym. I shouldn't even have to take gym in college anyway—dodgeball is for high school.*

Not that they actually played dodgeball in gym class. Well, maybe they did—he hasn't been to class often enough to notice what they do when they aren't in the actual classroom with desks. He thinks they go outside and run around the track sometimes. He always sneaks away at that point. He thought his vanishing act had gone unnoticed, but the C tells him otherwise.

Justin smirks, gearing up to face the Coach. He is charming. He knows how to do this. A few words, a few smiles, and that C will be an A in no time.

Coach Smith may run the athletics department at Abraxus Tasker College, and she may be in charge of the best football team the school has had in years, but she's still just a tiny red-headed woman. Justin is sure he can charm her.

He stands up after everyone else has left the room, debating which way to go to her office. He can cut through the locker room, which will probably be empty this time of morning since the teams don't usually practice until the afternoon, or he can go around through the hallway and come from the other side of the building. Justin decides that he doesn't want to walk around, just in case any other students are waiting in the hall to speak to the coach. From the locker room, he can see if anyone is there and wait out of sight until they leave. He doesn't want her to expect him, to prepare herself to see him. He knows he is sexy, knows that his female teachers are susceptible to flattery, and he's not above using the advantage of his good looks to get his way.

His twin sister Jamie can be the righteous one, insisting on earning her grades. Justin knows that given grades are far sweeter than earned grades, and he checks himself in the locker room mirror once more.

His face is handsome, strong cheekbones and black hair, dark eyes and sexy lips, and his body is just muscled enough to impress without being overbearing. He is young and strong and often sexy. This should be easy.

He knocks on the door to the coach's office, waiting for her low voice to tell him to enter before opening the door. Tightening his muscles to present a strong core, he steps into the room confidently, shutting the door behind him so no one else can hear their conversation. The closed blinds over the window rattle as the door closes, the sound loud as he turns around.

Coach Smith sits behind a metal desk covered in binders and papers, a computer monitor nearly buried in the chaos. Two chairs sit in front of her desk, and she gestures for him to sit in one of them. He obeys, looking behind her at the shelves of trophies, most of them decades old. The chair is comfortable as he sinks into it, and he resists the urge to sag. *It's gym class,* he reminds himself. *I need to show her I'm already in shape.*

"So Mr. Cooper," Coach Smith says, "what brings you to my office?"

"I wanted to talk about my grade," he begins, leaning forward with a charming smile.

"Of course you do," she sighs, grabbing a pile of papers and shuffling through it. She finds the page she is looking for and scans it with a delicate finger. "Ah yes, that's why."

"Why what?" he prompts.

"You have a 71%," she says. "That's a C." After a pause, she adds, "You realize that C is a gift, right? You're barely out of D range." She looks up. "You do know that class runs until 10:45?"

Justin nods. "Yeah."

"I wasn't sure," she comments, "since you tend to disappear around 10." She frowns at him. "I don't think I've ever seen you on the track, Mr. Cooper."

"I don't think I need to be on the track to stay in shape, Coach Smith," he replies, leaning forward to stretch out a toned forearm and rest it on the edge of her desk.

"The point of this class isn't about keeping your shape," she says, arching an eyebrow.

"Then what is the point of gym class in college?" he asks. He realizes it's the wrong thing to say immediately, watching as her eyes narrow at him.

"You might know that if you'd ever actually looked at the syllabus," she says tartly, glancing over his shoulder at the clock above the door.

Justin knows he has to do something quickly before he loses control of the conversation completely.

"I know that the syllabus covers the grade breakdown," he says quickly, "but it doesn't mention your extra credit policy."

Coach Smith looks at him again. "You angling for extra credit, Mr. Cooper?" she asks. "How original."

"So you've done it before," he presses.

"You mean let students do something completely extra that I then have to grade instead of just doing whatever the class assignments were?" she asks sweetly, her annoyance bleeding through the words.

"I can do anything," he offers, smiling just enough to suggest how far he is willing to go. "Anything you need."

She glances around the room. "I'm afraid I don't find myself needing anything at the moment," she says finally. She cocks her head. "I did need you to stay in class the whole time," she comments. She squints at him, face suddenly speculative. "Are you always a quick deserter or do you ever go the distance?"

Justin stares at her, mouth falling open. *Did she just…?*

Coach Smith chuckles, "That's what I thought." She looks him up and down, those bright eyes lingering on the lines of his shoulders and chest. "No doubt you always finish in a hurry," she tells him.

"I've never had any complaints," he defends himself, his bruised ego rallying. "I go the exact distance I need to go."

She scoffs. "Hardly." She pins him with a glare normally reserved for lazy athletes. "I bet you can't even manage to get me anywhere without losing it first." She sighs wistfully, looking over him at the clock again. "I really feel for some of these college girls," she admits, "stuck with such eager selfish boys."

"I can go the distance," Justin says, leaning forward now, face determined. "I can get you there and back again easily. No problem."

Coach Smith smiles at him, leaning back in her chair and spreading her legs suggestively. The short skirt she wears rides up to reveal delightfully creamy thighs, her skin smooth and taut. She puts one foot up on the edge of the desk, her sneaker pressed against the metal, and the skirt slides up even more, just enough to reveal her bare pussy to his suddenly lustful gaze.

"No problem?" she echoes, running a finger down her body to skim across her exposed skin. "You think you can get me off twice before you lose it?"

Justin bites his lip, nodding eagerly. He's always wanted to fuck Coach Smith. The tiny redhead has featured in more than one of his highlight reels. He glances over his shoulder at the closed door behind him, then over at the blinds pulled down over the glass window into the hallway. They are alone.

He scoots forward off the chair onto his knees, crawling behind the desk to kneel in front of her chair, aware of how she watches his body move across the floor, cool eyes assessing his muscles. He looks down at her bare pussy, the skin smooth and waxed. He's wondered if she is a true redhead since the first time he saw her months ago. Now he will never know.

"So what do I get if I succeed?" he asks, reaching out a hand to stroke her left leg, fingers sliding from the top of her socks, over her muscled calf, behind her knee, and lingering against her inner thigh.

Coach Smith smirks at him. "Tell you what," she says. "Get me off twice before you come, and I will just give you that A."

Justin lets his fingers slide up to graze the top of her clit, eyes focused on her expression. He nods, "Done."

"But if you don't," she adds, eyes pinning his, "you have to be my mascot for the rest of the season."

Justin's fingers falter, a frown crossing his handsome face. "What?"

"You heard me," Coach Smith says, grabbing his hand and pressing it against her clit, positioning his finger right where she wants it. "I need someone to be the mascot at the games," she tells him. "That's you."

Justin smirks, "But only if I come before you do." He leans forward, his free hand moving up her other leg, confident fingers finding her opening and sliding across her sensitive skin.

Coach Smith nods, "That's right." She lets go of his hand, reaching out to lift up his shirt instead, fingers opening the button of his jeans and pulling the zipper down.

"But—" Justin sputters, but then she is tugging his semi-hard cock from his boxers, small fingers wrapping around him in a way that makes him close his eyes and moan. He catches himself, then opens his eyes and bites his lip. "That's not fair," he accuses.

Coach Smith strokes his cock again, one hand focusing on the head and the other slipping down to cup his balls. "Who said this would be fair?" she breathes, a challenge in her eyes. "You need to earn at least twenty percent more for your grade here. That shouldn't be easy."

Justin rallies, and it is clear he knows his business, at least in theory, because he immediately goes to work with both hands, his thumb slowly stroking her clit in round lazy circles and his other fingers slide back and forth against her opening. "You are so wet," he moans, the thought making his cock get even harder in her grip. He wants to bury himself in that pussy, to pound her until the coach screams his name. But this is a challenge, and he means to succeed. Trying to focus around her hands on his cock, he watches her face for clues, reading the way her mouth opens in a low moan of pleasure as he continues to rub her clit, the red flush working its way up her chest as he slides one finger inside her.

"You make me wet," she tells him encouragingly. "But can you make me come?"

"Oh yeah, baby," he promises, shifting so that he has two fingers inside of her and rubs her clit with his thumb, his other hands pushing her shirt up, the purple and silver Stallions tank top revealing small but perky breasts with hard nipples. He leans forward to suck a nipple into his mouth, letting his other hand continue up to her neck and then her jaw, sliding a finger into her mouth. She sucks the finger, eagerly tasting herself on his skin, and presses against him, clearly wanting more. The rhythm on his cock falters, and he focuses, adding a third finger and increasing the speed of his thumb, keeping the pressure the same. He moves to the other nipple, sucking hard, and then moves up to trace the edge of her jaw.

She rocks against his hand, biting her lip, one hand abandoning his balls and sliding up to grab his neck, the other continuing that same sultry rhythm at the head of his cock. He needs to distract her from that, or he's going to lose this bet before he even begins.

"You like that?" he asks, kissing along her jaw, moving his hand faster. She scoots forward, body moving against him now.

"That's nice," she admits, opening her eyes to look at him, "Very nice." She moans, but the sound isn't right. She's enjoying herself, no doubt, but there's no more build up. Justin knows he will have to try a new angle.

"But you need more," he tells her, his mouth finding hers and sucking her lower lip into his. His tongue brushes against hers, skilled and eager. "I have more for you, baby."

"You better," she tells him, "or you're my mascot." She pauses. "Maybe you'll fuck better in the costume."

"I don't need a costume for this." He grins, kissing down her chin and neck, taking a moment to suck each nipple on his way down, then he leans forward to bury his face between her thighs. She loses her grip on his cock, finally breaking the rhythm that was going to break him, as he slides down onto the floor. He keeps his fingers moving inside her, gently sliding back and forth, and he sucks her clit, first hard then gently, the alternating rhythm eliciting gasps of pleasure from the coach.

"Oh fuck!" she says. "You do know how to lick pussy!"

He grins against her skin, unable to stop himself, feeling a little bit of pre-cum dribble out of the end of his cock at her words. He does have some skills, he thinks, tongue working in that same rhythm, loving how her little body is tight with eagerness. He feels the orgasm build, her pussy tightening around his fingers, body shuddering against him. He continues sucking on her clit for another moment while she moans, "Oh yes, Mr. Cooper!"

One down, he thinks. *One to go.* His cock is dripping. He pauses for a short moment breathing against her skin, then licks her again, knowing she will be sensitive. He leans forward to suck on her clit again, but she scoots forward, pushing off the chair and standing, her pussy pink and swollen but above him now. She crooks her finger, gesturing for him to stand up. He obeys, his pants pooling around his ankles, cock hard at attention. He wants to reach for her, knowing he could lift her easily, bring her down on his cock and fuck his way to glory.

But I need that A. Not yet, he tells himself. *One more.*

"Nicely done," she says, "but can you do it under duress?"

He raises an eyebrow, a hand absently pumping his cock as he stands in front of her. "What do you have in mind?"

She looks him over with a critical eye. "You say you don't need gym class," she says, "because you're already fit?"

Justin shrugs, knowing his body is nice to look at, but he is also strong and in shape. He could run on the track, but he just doesn't want to, preferring to run on the treadmill in the air conditioning at the gym with his music in his ears, not sweating under the sun with his classmates. "I am," he says. "What do you have in mind?" He imagines her climbing him like a tree, impaling that sweet pussy on his aching cock, breasts bouncing as she rides him like a wild woman, red hair a messy curtain around her flushed face.

"A challenge," she says, sliding her skirt and shirt off quickly. Justin takes off his shirt, dropping it onto her abandoned chair as she reaches for him. For a second, he thinks she is going to do exactly what he has been hoping, but instead of settling her legs around his hips, she turns him around so she stands next to his right side. She pats his shoulder to make sure he is steady on his feet, then reaches out to place both of her hands on top of his right shoulder. Like a cheerleader starting the bottom of a tower formation, she launches herself up with a bounce and lands on his shoulder in a surprising display of agility and strength, one leg against his chest and the other touching his back.

For a moment, she hovers there, her wet pussy pressed against his skin, and then she slowly slides around to his front, one thigh on either side of his face, her legs tucked over his shoulders and her pussy right in front of his mouth. She looks down at him, grinning, a hand on the back of his head. "You good so far?"

"Oh yeah," he says, tongue reaching out to lick her clit right in front of him, hands gripping that fantastic ass. He is strong enough to hold her like this for a while.

"Good," she says, "now hold on to me." His hands grip her ass and then slide to her waist and hips as she slowly leans back and down, body facing away from him to give him a great view of her breasts as she dangles from his shoulders like a cheerleader about to flip. But instead of lifting her legs from his shoulders and bouncing away from him, she lets herself straighten out upside down, making sure he has a good hold on her hips, her back pressed against his chest and stomach.

Justin moves her forward a little bit, angling her body so his tongue can reach all of the best parts of her. He is just settling into this new position, when the coach shifts, twisting her upper body around so that one hand grips his right thigh and her other hand cups his balls while warmth enfolds his cock. He freezes, hips jerking forward involuntarily as she sucks him deep into her warm mouth, his tongue slipping back into his mouth as he moans. She pulls him close again, this time squeezing his balls in a steady rhythm to match her mouth, and Justin knows he isn't going to make it.

He leans forward, diving into her pussy with his tongue, but she keeps sucking his cock in that perfect rhythm, hands pressing his balls in the same motion. He pulls her hips forward again, burying his tongue in her, and while he knows that she is close to coming again, there is no way he is going to outlast that mouth on his cock.

His mind races through possible ways to stop himself from coming, all of the things that could stop the wave of pleasure, but her mouth is moving in a way that makes him see stars, and he steps awkwardly back, leaning his butt against her desk. A binder crashes to the floor but he ignores it, licking her pussy with everything in him.

The wave builds even higher, and he knows he won't be able to hold it.

How bad could the mascot really be? Justin decides he can suffer through a few games in a silly suit if only he can come in that magic mouth right now.

He lets go with a moan, sucking her clit in a last desperate effort, and then he collapses onto the desk behind him, careful not to bend his body too much and hurt the coach as she sucks the orgasm out of him. She uses a hand on the desk to prop herself up, then easily sits up in front of his face. She looks down at him, a hand in his hair as she swallows, licking a finger suggestively.

"Oh no," she croons, shaking her head. "Like I thought, too soon across the finish line."

"That was a dirty trick," he says against her pussy, tongue snaking out to lick her again.

"That was just a blowjob," she tells him.

"I've had blowjobs," Justin says. "That was … athletics."

Coach Smith snorts, lifting a leg off his shoulder and climbing off of him. "I am the Director of Athletics," she reminds him. "You should expect that kind of thing." She steps back into her skirt, then slides her tank top over her head, shaking her hair out over the neck. Justin leans down to pull up his pants, grabs his shirt from where he abandoned it on the chair, and stands there, still catching his breath.

"So," Coach Smith says dismissively, leaning down to pick up the binder from the floor and adding it to the top of a haphazard pile near the edge. "Game is Friday at 7. I expect you in the locker room at 6."

2

ustin Cooper stares at the mascot costume laid out on the bench, debating how to begin. He glances hopefully at the few guys in the locker room with him. They've probably seen people put this on before. Maybe they can help.

He picks up the bottom, studying the structure of the costume. He's wearing gym shorts and a tank top, so it should be easy enough to slide the pants over his legs. Stepping into one leg, he wobbles a little, arm reaching out to catch his balance on the bench, but a strong arm grabs his shoulder and holds him steady.

Justin looks over his shoulder to see Aaron, the quarterback for the XTC Stallions grinning at him. "You got roped into the mascot, huh?" he asks, nodding sympathetically. "What did you do to piss someone off?"

"It's extra credit," Justin tells him. "For gym."

Aaron nods slowly, a flash of understanding passing between them. "Coach can be a real hard-ass sometimes," he says. "Very demanding woman." He bites his lip, shaking his head as his eyes go distant, lost in memory. Seeming to return to the moment, he gestures with his chin. "I'll hold you up. Once you get the other leg on and get the shoulders the right length, you should be fine." He holds Justin's shoulder steady, allowing the smaller man to slide his other leg into the furred costume. The waist lifts easily, and

Justin finds two shoulder straps tucked inside. He pulls them out and Aaron helps him adjust the height so the costume sits on his actual waist. As he pulls the second strap over his shoulder, something rolls out of the middle section of the costume and lands at his crotch. Justin looks down inside the costume, confused, and then surprised to see what looks like a dildo.

"No way," he breathes, snaking his arm inside the costume to pull it out. In the fluorescent lights of the locker room, he can see that it is about eight inches long and purple with a large wide base for easy gripping or using in a strap-on. He holds it up, looking at Aaron curiously. "Um?"

Aaron laughs, pushing his hand down and jamming the dildo back inside the costume. The quarterback smirks. "I'd just put that back where you found it," he says.

"Is this some kind of joke?" Justin asks, sliding the dildo back into a small pocket along the inside of the costume. The chest is larger than his own, loosely framed so there is plenty of room for the dildo without him feeling it. "Do I want to know?"

"Different strokes for different folks," Aaron says cryptically.

"Who wore this before me?"

"Someone who clearly liked to have a good time," Aaron says with a shrug. "I'd leave it alone."

Justin laughs, looking down at the furred costume covering him to mid chest. "I probably should have pissed before I got into this," he grumbles.

"No worries, mate," Aaron tells him, leaning down to flick a flap of fabric across the costume's crotch. "There's a flap here. Makes it much easier."

"That dildo suddenly makes a lot more sense," Justin comments, feeling around to get a sense of the flap. He has to pull down the horse's sewn-on gym shorts to access it, but there's plenty of room for his cock to go through it if he needs to.

Aaron frowns. "It also lets you get a breeze inside the costume occasionally. It's not too hot tonight, but sometimes that thing can be brutal." The quarterback gestures at the rest of the costume—a long-sleeved shirt of brown fur wearing a purple and silver Stallions jersey and a horse head fitted with what feels like a helmet inside. "You got this part or you need help?"

Justin nods. "I got this," he tells him. "But can you tell me if it's okay when it's all on?"

"Sure."

Justin reaches for the shirt, pleased to find that it doesn't smell bad when he tugs it over his head. They must have the costume cleaned regularly. He adjusts the shoulders, surprised to find that the material isn't that heavy. It's like a winter coat, and not entirely uncomfortable. He tugs the plush horse head over his head, glad to see that it's easy to see out through the mouth. His fingers fumble for the clips to secure the head to the rest of the costume, and then everything settles into place. He jumps a little, testing the movement.

"Not bad," Aaron nods. "Can you do the dance?"

Justin sighs, but he steps away from the bench, launching into the hip-thrusting jig the mascot makes at every goal.

"That'll do," Aaron says, grabbing his shoulders and pointing him at the doorway to the practice field and beyond. "Go get 'em, Stallion. Eager fans await your presence!"

*J*ustin raises his arms in a huge clap, rocking his hips in the goal dance as the Stallions score yet another touchdown. The crowd screams, the stadium echoing with excitement.

"And that's another victory for your XTC Stallions!" the announcer yells, and the crowd lets out another cheer. Justin pumps his fists, arms only starting to hurt from the evening's exertions. He didn't realize how much the mascot moved around during a game, jumping and dancing and keeping the crowd going the entire time.

He is absolutely earning his extra points with all of this. He really wants to reach inside the horse's mouth and brush his sweaty hair out of his face, but he doesn't want to freak out any of the kids in the audience.

The game ends with a final whistle, and Justin spends the next half hour giving high fives and posing for selfies as the crowd slowly leaves the stands. The players are long gone, disappeared to the locker room for showers and gone to the after party. Justin thinks he can probably go to the celebration and debates how tired he is. He does not miss the irony that his extra credit for gym class is definitely a workout.

When no one else remains in the stands, he makes his way slowly back to the locker room. There is still steam in the air, remnants of the last showers, but the room is empty, a few stray towels lingering on the benches for someone else to pick up. Justin walks over to the bench and sits down, legs relieved to rest after the constant motion of the last three hours. He finds the buckles connecting the horse head to his shoulders and releases one. One arm is still inside the costume when a stern voice makes him freeze.

"Did I say you were finished, Mr. Cooper?"

Justin snaps his head up, the horse head lolling a bit to one side as one buckle is undone, but Coach Smith doesn't seem to mind. She is elated, her face glowing in satisfaction. She still wears her ball cap over that glorious red hair and a purple and silver jacket over her normal shirt and skirt.

"What else do you need, Coach Smith?" His hand moves to his pants, sliding down the waistband of his shorts.

She studies him, lips pursing as she takes a few slow steps closer to where he sits. She takes off her hat first, letting it fall to the floor and releasing her hair in a wave. Justin stares at her, cock growing hard at the memory of their last encounter.

"I'm not sure you're up to the task," she says with a frown, a finger lingering on the zipper of her jacket. She tugs it down slowly, and Justin grows harder as he realizes that she must have taken off her shirt at some point during the evening, the jacket falling aside to reveal two bare breasts with tight nipples. He remembers how she wasn't wearing panties when he went to visit her in the office, and he hopes she is bare this time too. He grips his cock, pulling it free of his shorts and giving a few short pumps.

"I can do anything you need me to," he promises, voice husky through the mask.

"I think you might do better without as much stimulation," she says, sliding the jacket off slowly, knowing his eyes are on every inch of revealed skin. "Let's see how well you can control yourself." The jacket hits the floor, and she stands in front of him wearing a tiny white pleated skirt. "A little test first, though." She reaches down, easily sliding the costume's shorts out of the way and lifting the strategically placed flap. Justin is expecting her, so his cock stands free of his own shorts, poking proudly through the hole in the costume.

She nods approvingly. "A promising start," she says, "but that was true last time too." She frowns. "Can you handle a little more excitement?" She turns around, lifting her skirt slowly to reveal first the long lines of her thighs and finally the curve of her ass. Justin's cock jerks in response to the sight, a drop of pre-cum shiny on the tip. She turns to frown down at him, shaking her head. "Mr. Cooper, you must control yourself."

"I am," he insists, "but you are so fucking hot right now."

Coach Smith smiles at him, a finger in her mouth as she sucks the tip. "You cannot cum yet," she demands.

"Yes, ma'am," he replies, steeling himself.

She lifts a long leg, draping it over the bench and wrapping it around the back of the costume. She lowers herself slowly onto his cock, her other leg stretching over his to kneel on the bench. Justin moans as her warmth enfolds him, his free arm reaching around to feel her breasts. She knocks his arm down as she settles herself on his cock. "No," she tells him. "No touching. Just this."

Justin closes his eyes, not wanting to lose the sight of her breasts through the opening of the horse's mouth, but unable to focus on anything but the feel of that warm pussy on his cock, the only part of her touching his body. It's an odd sensation. He can feel her weight on his legs, the motion of the costume's fabric as she slowly moves up and down, but he can't feel any part of her except the warm tightness over his cock.

"Fucking christ," he moans, hand lifting again to touch her as he opens his eyes to watch the beautiful woman riding him. She grabs the arm and pins it to his side, using it to hold as she moves up and down a little faster, breasts rising and falling with each bounce.

"Fucking Coach," she corrects, leaning back with her eyes closed, relishing the moment.

"Yes, ma'am," he says again, soaking in the sight as she leans back a little, breasts bouncing more as she increases her speed again. Justin can tell she is close to the edge, and he slides his other hand down again, slipping it out of the flap just enough for his thumb to press against her clit the next time she slides down his cock. Her eyes fly open and she stares at him through the mask, grinding her hips against his thumb with each thrust down.

"You naughty boy!" she exclaims, driving her body onto his cock. "You're going to make me cum!" she yells, body shuddering against his. She pumps her hips a few more times, then sags against him, breath ragged as she sits, his hard cock still deep inside of her. "Nicely done, Mr. Cooper," she tells him when she sits up, wrapping her other leg around his hip and hooking her feet over his butt.

"I think you've earned a little reward," she says. "What would you like for your efforts?"

Justin stands up, snaking his hand outside of the costume so he can use both arms to hold her steady on his cock as he maneuvers around the costume, trying to get a feel for the weight distribution. "I want to fuck you silly," he says, spinning around and taking a few steps to press her back against the locker room wall. The motion makes it much easier to hold her, the costume bunched up just enough to hold her in place as he moves his hips for a slow first thrust back and forth. She lets out a moan, head ducked into the shoulder of the costume.

Justin squares his feet, settling into a medium pace, letting the friction build again as he pumps into her. "Fuck you are so tight," he moans.

"That cock is so big," she says. "And you move just right!"

"Are you going to cum on this big cock?" he asks, thrusting from a slightly different angle. The noise she makes lets him know he has found the spot, and he focuses his efforts on hitting it every time he slides into her.

"Keep doing that!" she demands, body clinging to his, muscles trembling as she approaches the edge again. "Fuck yes!" she yells, body convulsing around his.

Justin nearly loses it, but he manages to hold himself back, thrusting a few more times as she squeezes him tight and then holding her steady, letting her shuddering body relax.

"Well done, Mr. Cooper," she says in a ragged voice. "I didn't think you had it in you."

"I believe it's in you, Coach Smith," he says, lifting her away from the wall and allowing her to slide off his cock to slowly stand on shaky legs. "Or it will be," he adds, hands on her shoulders to push her gently down on the bench. She kneels, perfect ass facing him as her skirt flips up over her hips. She turns around to see him, eyes dark over her shoulder and she bites her lip.

"Fuck me again, Mr. Cooper," she demands. "And this time, you're allowed to come. But only after I do."

"Greedy woman," Justin tells her, stepping forward to grab the line of her skirt, using the material to tug her ass back to him, her wet pussy enfolding his hard cock. He looks down, marveling at the idea of his cock inside of his teacher, the costume still between them. She presses back against him, moaning as he pulls back and watches his cock disappear inside her pussy again, pink lips sliding along the shaft. "Is this what you want?" he demands, pounding into her harder, losing sight of his cock as he looks up over the curve of her ass to see her head, hair in disarray over her face. "You like this cock, Coach Smith?"

"Oh yes!" she cries, ass pushing back against him. "Fuck me with that cock, Mr. Cooper!"

He uses one hand on the skirt to set the rhythm, pleasure building in his lower belly, then smacks her ass with the other, goading her on to move faster, harder. Finally, he lets go, pounding into her with abandon, both of them shouting their pleasure. Her body shudders around him, and he jerks, pouring himself deep inside of her as he comes. He pauses, then sags forward, body awkwardly draped over her back as he waits for his heart to calm back down to normal pace.

"Well, Mr. Cooper," she breathes, "it turns out you can go the distance on occasion."

4

"I cannot believe I'm doing this," Jamie Cooper complains, walking through the sliding doors into the XTC Stallions Athletic Center. "Twin brothers are the absolutely worst. He so owes me one for this. Big time."

She scans the entryway, glad to see that no one is around. Justin insisted that she wouldn't be seen at this time. She could come in, grab the costume, get dressed for the game on Friday back in her room, and cover for him so he could get his A in gym class.

"I can't believe you agreed to be the mascot," she told her brother. "That seems like a lot more effort than you normally put forth."

"You'd be surprised," Justin replied, smirking with some hidden joke. Jamie doesn't want to know. She wants to get into the locker room, grab the costume, and get back to her room before anyone notices.

She opens the locker room door slowly, listening intently for any noise. Hearing none, she steps inside, sneakers quiet on the tile floor. The mascot costume sits where Justin said it would be, propped up on the corner of the bench across the room, the horse head sitting next to the other pieces. Frowning, Jamie considers the costume. She can put it on and walk across campus without too much comment. There isn't a game until tomorrow, but Justin can't let any of the players see that he has his sister covering for him, so she needs to get into costume elsewhere.

She listens for another moment, hearing nothing, and walks closer to the costume. Lifting the pants, she frowns again.

Justin, you owe me big time, she thinks with a sigh, putting the costume on the ground and stepping into one leg. She wobbles dangerously when she tries to put in her other leg but catches herself against the bench just in time. The shoulder straps are the right height—she and Justin are the same size—so it's easy to put them on. She tugs the shirt over her head, pleasantly surprised by the fresh smell. They must dry clean the costume often.

She adjusts the shirt, then finds the clips along the shoulders, no doubt meant to connect to the head. Sighing, she lifts up the head, staring into the long partially open mouth.

"Fuck my life," she groans, resting the head on top of her own, balancing the awkward weight. She finds one clip and secures a side, but then there are voices just outside the door.

Jamie panics, not sure what to do. In a flurry, she whirls around to face the door. The weight of the costume knocks her off balance and she stumbles backward, landing awkwardly in the corner of the room, but landing heavily on the bench. The horse head slides to one side and she slides her arms inside the costume to catch it, not caring if the shoulder straps fall off her shoulders. The shirt covers her body. She drags the head back into place and then sags back, praying that the costume looks like someone left it that way on purpose, leaning into the corner, as the door opens.

A blonde girl walks in, flanked by three men, clearly players. Jamie recognizes the twins Bryan and Ryan from her sociology class. The third guy is vaguely familiar, like she's seen him at the Tutoring Center before, but she can't place his name.

Fuck, she thinks, watching the group as they chat for a moment, something about studying for finals, body tense as she stays motionless inside the costume. *Good, if they're getting ready to go study, they won't stay very long.*

Her hopes for a quick exit are dashed when Aaron, the gorgeous quarterback who has starred in more than one of her shower fantasies, comes inside. His words make something quiver deep inside Jamie. She doesn't believe what she sees at first, sure that her oversexed mind is reading into the body language of the people in the gym, but when Aaron leans in and asks, "What do you think?" in that sexy voice, Jamie wants to scream at the propositioned blonde, "Say yes! Dear god say yes!"

The eight guys surround the blonde and lead her into the shower, presumably a reward for her getting the answer on her study card right.

Oh wow, Jamie thinks, not really believing what she's seeing until Aaron leans down to kiss her while the big guy slides his hands into the girl's pants. Her own hand drifts lower on her belly, wishing she could have so many hands on her body at one time. The two guys undress the blonde, revealing a body that makes Jamie question her orientation. She's made out with girls before, but she tends to prefer cock—this woman might satisfy her without one.

Jamie's hand moves lower, sliding along the edge of her gym shorts, teasing her skin as she watches. When the boys carry the girl—Bree, she knows now, she's heard them whisper her name a few times—into the shower and she begins stroking the redhead's cock, Jamie sighs, shifting her body slightly so she can get her hand inside of her pants. Her touch is gentle at first, teasing as she watches Bree stroke the men in the shower, taking turns kissing them. But when Aaron kneels to bury his face in the blonde's pussy, Jamie's hand becomes more insistent, pressing hard with a soft jerk against the side of the mascot, and something falls out of a pocket to tumble onto her lap. Jamie freezes, wondering if anyone saw the movement.

Desperate cries echo from the shower, and she sighs in relief, knowing that no one would be watching this side of the room with that show in front of them. She's fascinated too.

Her hand pulls out of her pants, curious about the object that she dislodged. Her fingers locate the soft silky texture of a long firm object, and she drops the item in shock. It lands against her belly, surface silicone smooth, and she reaches for it again, surprise giving way to excitement.

Of course, she thinks. *Of course there's a dildo inside the mascot. Why wouldn't there be?*

She turns her attention back to the shower, angling her head so she can see around the bulk of the twins who stand partially blocking the opening. She can see that the girl is on the floor now, head thrown back as her body moves rhythmically, no doubt fucking one of the lucky players. Jamie's hand snakes inside her pants again, imagining that she is in that shower, men surrounding her as she rides Aaron's cock all the way home. Her body grows tight, and she closes her eyes, caught in the fantasy as her fingers press hard against her clit. She holds in a moan as the pleasure builds, shuddering as the wave crashes over her, hand relaxing on her clit as the orgasm ebbs.

She opens her eyes again, this time seeing the woman held up by the guys, hands rubbing her body, a face buried between her thighs again. Jamie brushes against her clit again, watching intently, knowing that her second orgasm is always much faster and more powerful than the first. The pleasure floods her, and then she sags back.

The water turning off has her opening her eyes again, and she watches, expecting the party to be over. To her surprise, the guys carry the blonde over to the massage table, where she climbs to all fours so one player can fuck her while she sucks the other's cock.

Jamie's hand drifts over the dildo, wishing she could have a cock inside her too.

Oh no, she thinks wickedly. *I can't.*

But when the player flips Bree over and sheaths himself in one move, powerful body moving against hers, Jamie decides that she can. She moves the dildo slowly, sliding the length so it's even with her thighs at first, then slips it between her shorts and her leg, hiking up her shorts as she goes. The head is thick, but her pussy is wet when she reaches it, sliding her panties aside easily to rest the dildo against her opening.

Bree is moaning on the table, clearly about to come again, and Jamie presses the dildo in, just a little bit, letting her body accept the width. Her other hand moves to stroke her clit again, pressing down hard as she slowly moves on the dildo.

The players have swapped again, this time with one between Bree's legs while the other straddles her and fucks her gorgeous breasts. The other guys are kneeling around her, hands pumping hard cocks.

This is fucking amazing, Jamie thinks, squeezing her pussy on the dildo, taking a little more inside of her with each moan from the table. *Or amazing fucking!*

She is about to come, but then a door slams, and Coach Smith walks into the room. Jamie freezes, heart pounding, sure they are all going to get in trouble. But when the Coach simply climbs on the table to sit on Bree's face, Jamie loses control, sliding her small body up and down on the dildo and rubbing her clit furiously, coming hard and fast, her own pleasure lost in the general chorus of moans coming from the other side of the table.

Jamie recovers enough to hear Bree's last words: "Best. Studygroup. Ever." They don't take long after that, quick showers and friendly banter as they all head out of the locker room.

She waits until the room is empty, moving her stuff muscles slowly. She slides the dildo out of her pussy, echoes of pleasure streaking through her, and gets slowly to her feet.

Bree is so right. That was the best study session ever. Jamie doesn't think she will ever forget the names of the body systems with such excellent visual aids.

*J*amie raises her arms, encouraging the crowd to whoop in
time with the music as Aaron throws yet another winning
touchdown. She has been in the costume for a few hours, but no
one seems to notice that she isn't Justin. She is tired, her body in
shape but exhausted by the effort of moving the heavy horse head
around the crowd. She performs the dancing jig that accompanies
the goal, but the muscles in her stomach and thighs protest, not
used to the motion.

She can't wait to get back to the locker room and take off the
costume. She plans to leave it on the bench in the locker room,
slipping out unnoticed after the players finish up.

She lingers with the crowd after the game, giving Aaron's
blonde head a lingering gaze as he leaves the field, carried along
in the swell of his fans' adoration.

Someday, she thinks, *I will have that boy.*

With a sigh, she walks slowly back to the locker room, hoping
that the players will all be on to the afterparty by now. When she
walks in, the room is dark, the sensor lights turned off after a period
with no motion. Jamie sighs in relief, moving to the corner bench
where she found the mascot the first time she came in the locker
room. The lights turn on as she enters, the room flooded as she
moves, and Coach Smith is sitting on the bench in the corner, legs

spread wide along each length of wood, skirt flipped up to reveal her bare pussy. Her hands work slow circles on her clit, her skin flushed pink.

"You certainly took your time, Mr. Cooper," Coach Smith says with a languid smile. "I've done most of the work for you already."

Jamie freezes, knowing that she cannot speak or risk giving her brother away. *You freaking idiot*, she thinks angrily. *It's not enough that you dicked around and now need to be the mascot for the grade you need, but now you're fucking the teacher?* She takes a deep breath, squaring her shoulders inside the suit, knowing what her brother would do in this situation. They are twins, after all. Justin can't be that different from her in bed.

Fuck, she thinks, eyes widening as she takes a few steps toward the coach. *She's expecting me to fuck her again. I may be willing to go fairly far to help out my brother, but my willingness isn't going to give me a dick!*

She reaches the bench, appreciating the welcoming smile on Coach Smith's face. She's seen the coach join in on the gang bang with Bree, so she has an idea what the beautiful woman considers a good time. Jamie raises her arms to the horse head, undoing one of the straps and tilting the head to the side, moving it so the lower part of her face is visible through the mouth. The head is still shadowed, and they look enough alike that the coach should not be able to tell it's not Justin.

Dammit Justin, can't you just do your regular work? Now I have to earn your extra credit! As she takes in the lines of the coach's svelte body, Jamie decides that it's not a complete hardship. Coach Smith is smoking hot. Jamie is willing to take one for the team.

She gets to her knees, reaching out to caress the coach with her gloved hands, sliding the furry suit against the coach's slick wetness. Jamie suddenly knows why this suit smells so good. It must get cleaned fairly regularly after being used like this. She wonders how many students have worn it; how many have earned extra points by pleasuring the coach this way. Coach Smith moans, looking down at where Jamie kneels in appreciation. "Determined to get caught up, are we?" she asks. "Don't worry. I have plenty more left in me."

Jamie focuses on her work, rubbing her paws against the Coach the way she enjoys being touched, reading the woman's body for cues. Leaning down, she lifts one of the Coach's legs over her shoulder, bringing her mouth to the warm skin of her clit. It's not the first time she's licked pussy, and it probably won't be the last. Jamie enjoys sex of all kinds, though in the end, she prefers a good hard cock to end the encounter. She feels herself getting wet as she buries her tongue in the coach's slick folds, still using her hands to rub slow circles over her clit.

"Oh, Mr. Cooper!" Coach Smith yells. "You've been practicing!"

Jamie restrains a chuckle, her warm breath puffing out to stimulate the Coach's smooth skin, and she presses down on the clit more firmly, sensing the coach is close. She has wrapped her other leg around the back of Jamie's neck, the horse head sliding but not in danger of falling off as she presses closer.

Coach Smith moans as her body tightens, the orgasm spilling through her. Jamie gives her a moment to catch her breath, but then dives back in, knowing that the second orgasm is often easier than the first, and sometimes more powerful when combined with the effects of the first one so soon after. The coach stiffens against Jamie's mouth, coming again and shuddering against her face. She leans back after that, body falling limp to lean against the corner, small breasts heaving as she catches her breath.

"Mr. Cooper," she says after a moment, eyes narrowed, "you have been paying attention." She removes her leg from Jamie's shoulder and slides down to sit on Jamie's lap, eager mouth finding Jamie's under the mask, their heads tilted just enough so the coach can't see the rest of her face. Jamie returns the kiss, enjoying the coach's mouth, letting her hands slide over pert breasts and then down to hold her hips.

She drags out the kiss, mind frantically running through options for the next step. Coach Smith's hands begin working at the shorts, and Jamie remembers the dildo at the last second. She slides a hand back inside the costume, hoping the coach will think she's adjusting her clothes, and grabs the dildo, positioning it with her hand so it faces the right direction. She sucks the coach's tongue into her mouth as she does so, distracting the woman long enough for Jamie to slide the flap aside and use her hand to find her dripping pussy. The coach doesn't wait, following Jamie's hand back to slide down the length of the dildo, rocking her hips forward as she does so. The base of the dildo presses against Jamie's clit, and she stifles a moan. Her hand returns to the base, and she grips it hard, determined to keep the dildo steady as Coach Smith begins to move up and down.

The sight is delightful, Coach Smith's breasts bouncing up and down just below Jamie's eye level, her chest flushed with passion, soft gasps of pleasure escaping her lips as she increases her speed. "Cooper," she says, "you are so hard for me tonight!"

Jamie bites her lip, the pressure of the dildo base and her own hand rubbing her clit in all the right ways. She begins to breathe more heavily, and pitching her voice low like Justin's, she lets a small moan escape.

"Oh yes!" Coach Smith moans, body moving hard and fast now. "Come for me!"

Jamie rocks her hips up, hoping the coach will think Justin is coming, and she lets out a low hitching moan. Coach puts her hands on Jamie's shoulders and leans back, her entire body shuddering as she rides herself over the edge. Her body collapses against the furry chest of the costume, and they stay that way for a moment, both breathing hard—coach from her orgasm, Jamie from frustration. The dildo has gotten her close, but it's not enough. She needs just a little bit more.

Coach Smith stands up slowly, and Jamie is quick to yank the dildo back inside, folding the flap back into place before the woman can look down. The coach smiles, nods, and takes a few steps across the room. She turns back to where Jamie still kneels on the floor.

"Nicely done, Cooper," Coach Smith. "I think you've definitely earned that A!"

*J*amie waits for Coach Smith to leave the locker room, then stands up on shaky legs, turns around, and plops on the bench. She hears the door of the coach's office open and shut, and then there is no more noise. Jamie rests, catching her breath and letting her heart slow back down, very aware of the frustrated tension in her lower belly. She tucks the dildo back inside the suit, knowing that whoever gets it cleaned will take care of it, then rests her hand on top of her pussy, finger idly toying with her clit.

She contemplates rubbing herself to orgasm quickly, but then frowns. She really wants to get out of the costume. She abandons her clit, using both hands to undo the second clip on the horse head, and she takes it off with a sigh, her sweaty hair falling in her face as she rests it on the bench next to her.

"No fucking way," a voice says, and she jerks her head up to see Aaron, star quarterback and gorgeous blonde, staring at her from where he has entered the locker room. He narrows his eyes at her. "You're not Justin."

Jamie bites her lip, not sure what to say. She doesn't remember if Justin and Aaron are close friends or not.

Aaron looks from her to the hallway where the coach disappeared a while ago and then back at her. "You're not Justin," he says again, head cocking to the side, "but you just fucked Coach."

He pauses, then adds, "And did a damn good job of it, judging by her expression when she walked out of here."

Jamie smiles brightly at him, deciding to brazen it out. "I have some skills," she says.

"Does one of those skills involve a cock?" he asks. "Because I'm pretty sure she was riding you a little while ago."

Jamie looks down, biting her bottom lip hard, unable to speak, not sure what to say. She wasn't expecting her first conversation with Aaron to involve him asking if she had a cock. "I... uh... have lots of skills?" she says eventually, voice shy as she looks away.

Aaron chuckles, walking over to sit on the bench next to her. He leans back against the wall. "So you're Justin's sister, right? Jamie?"

Jamie smiles, surprised that he knows her name. She nods. "And you're Aaron," she says.

He looks her up and down in the costume, a slow grin crossing his face. "Wanna tell me what's going on?"

Jamie shrugs. "Brothers are a huge pain in the ass?"

Aaron laughs. "True. But sisters are awesome," he says, flashing her a charming smile, "especially smoking hot ones."

Jamie raises an eyebrow, not buying it. Her hair is plastered to her head from wearing the horse head. Her mouth is still shiny with Coach Smith's wetness. She's flushed and flustered and sitting in most of a mascot costume next to the object of her crush.

"Yeah, right," she says, rolling her eyes and running a hand through her hair. "Nothing about me is smoking right now."

"You are a delicious hot mess," he says, leaning closer to her. "But you must be dying in that costume. How about I help you take it off?"

Jamie nods, face warming at the idea of Aaron helping her take off any kind of clothing.

He turns to her, grabbing her arm first and sliding off one glove. He sets it to the side then scoots closer to her, hands reaching for her other arm, and making a face when he realizes that one of her sleeves is empty, the hand already inside the costume. "Arms up?" he suggests, and Jamie lifts her one arm, letting him tug the shirt over her head. She sighs with relief as the cool air hits her flushed skin, setting the shirt on the bench next to the rest of the costume. "Better?" he asks.

"Much," she nods, but looks down at herself. "But I need to get out of the rest of this."

"Happy to help," he says, moving closer to slide the shoulder strap off her arm, hands lingering on her skin as he moves it down. He pushes the other strap to the side, and the costume sinks, falling to puddle around her waist. Jamie lifts both arms up, stretching tired muscles, and Aaron moves closer, grabbing her gently about the hips and tugging her legs up on the bench, sliding her body so she now sits with her back to one wall, the left side of her body touching the other wall. He slides the pants off one leg at a time, helping to lift her hips off the bench so the costume can slip free. Jamie is very aware of what she is wearing underneath, a simple tank top and small bootie shorts.

Aaron smiles at her, tossing the remains of the costume on top of the pile on the other side of her. "Better?"

"Definitely."

He lifts both of her legs so they rest on top of his lap, scooting closer on the bench until he turns his body, and leans forward, a hand capturing her chin and tilting her face up to him.

"You are so hot," he breathes. "Can I kiss you?"

"Fuck yeah," Jamie says, closing the distance between their faces, mouth claiming his fiercely, knowing that she still tastes of Coach Smith's pussy, knowing that Aaron will enjoy her kiss even more. She puts a hand on the back of his neck, pulling him closer and urging him on, the frustration in her body surging to the surface. One of his hands slides down from her face to cup the outside of her shoulder and then slides down her arm, moving more slowly as he gets near her breasts.

The heat in Jamie's belly pulses, and she grabs his hand and jams it to her breast, encouraging him even more. He pulls away slightly, breath still a whisper on her lips, "You want me?"

"I want you to fuck me sideways and silly," she tells him, biting his lower lip with hers. "I'm so fucking horny right now. I need you inside of me!"

Aaron grins, hands slipping down to tug off her shorts.

"Happy to help!" His hands return to her pussy immediately, sliding against her wet heat. "Fuck, Jamie," he moans, burying fingers inside of her slick warmth.

"Yes," she tells him, "please fuck Jamie."

He grins again, hand moving faster, breath against her mouth. "I am so glad you don't have a cock right now."

"No cock yet," she tells him, hands reaching to tug his pants off, "but I hope to have one soon." She pauses long enough to let him take off his shirt, hands tugging from behind his neck in that adorable way men always take off shirts. His clothes land on the floor, and then she is climbing on top of him. She wants to ride him the way the coach rode her dildo.

He stops her with firm hands on her hips, sliding her closer to him, her bare thighs rubbing against the tops of his legs, and his huge cock is hard, shaft rubbing against her clit as she presses her body close to his. She leans back as he scoots forward a little bit, giving her legs enough room to wrap around his waist.

Aaron leans forward, claiming her mouth again, rubbing his cock against the front of her pussy, the hard muscles of his abdomen pressing against her soft skin, his hand sliding up to pinch a nipple, the other reaching around to grip her ass. "You want this cock?" he asks, and Jamie moans in response.

"Please," she says finally, body aching with need.

He lifts her easily, hands guiding her body as she slips down the length of his shaft, the burning desire inside finally getting what she wants. "Yes," she says, moving her body slowly, relishing the feeling of fullness, the promise of satisfaction after so much buildup and tension. She moves slowly at first, hands holding his shoulders to help her set the rhythm, eager mouth moving against his. She finds a speed she likes and leans in close, releasing his mouth long enough to cry out her release.

"There you go," he says as she shudders against him. When she comes back to herself, he gives her a challenging grin. "I'm thinking about five more of those, and we should be somewhere close to where we need to be," he tells her.

"Only five?" she teases. "Why not six? That's a touchdown, at least."

Aaron smirks. "Then I should go for the extra point and call it seven," he promises, hands gripping her ass.

Jamie smiles at him, body beginning to move again. "Sounds good," she says, squeezing him tight inside. "And I expect every single one of them. Call it my extra credit."

ALI WHIPPE

li Whippe loves trying new delights, especially of the non-vanilla variety. Her obsession with naughty words and sexy situations is only topped by her need to push the boundaries in every possible way. While her XTC and Honey Pot series play with all things wicked and sultry, the Collectors series is her first foray into paranormal erotica, and she never knew the world of magic and fantasy could be so deliciously sinful. She hopes you enjoy the ride as much as she did.

MORE BOOKS BY ALI WHIPPE
Office Hours
Tutoring Center
Athletics
Extra Credit

Bound for Release
Fetish Circuit
Now You See Me
Sexual Playground

Swingers

Discovered

XTC College Series Collection

More books from 4 Horsemen Publications

Erotica

Aria Skylar
Twisted Eros
Seducing Dionysus

Chastity Veldt
Molly in Milwaukee
Irene in Indianapolis
Lydia in Louisville
Natasha in Nashville
Alyssa in Atlanta
Betty in Birmingham
Carrie on Campus
Jackie in Jacksonville
A Humorous Erotica Collection

Dalia Lance
My Home on Whore Island
Slumming It on Slut Street
Training of the Tramp
The Imperfect Perfection
Spring Break
72% Match
It Was Meant To Be... Or Whatever

Honey Cummings
Sleeping with Sasquatch

Cuddling with Chupacabra
Naked with New Jersey Devil
Laying with the Lady in Blue
Wanton Woman in White
Beating it with Bloody Mary
The Erotic Cryptid Collection
Beau and Professor Bestialora
The Goat's Gruff
Goldie and Her Three Beards
Pied Piper's Pipe
Princess Pea's Bed
Pinocchio and the Blow Up Doll
Jack's Beanstalk
Pulling Rapunzel's Hair
The Urban Erotica Fairy
Tale Collection
Curses & Crushes
Queen's Incubus

Nick Savage
The Fairlane Incidents
The Fortunate Finn Fairlane
The Fragile Finn Fairlane
The Complete Package

Keep reading at
4HorsemenPublications.com

Pine Valley Series : Book Four

DREAMER

ON THE

MOUNTAIN

CORRINE ARDOIN

Black Rose Writing | Texas

The author grants the final approval for this literary material.

First printing

This is a work of fiction. Names, characters, businesses, places, events,
and incidents are either the products of the author's imagination or
used in a fictitious manner. Any resemblance to actual persons, living or
dead, or actual events is purely coincidental.

ISBN: 978-1-68513-249-1
PUBLISHED BY BLACK ROSE WRITING
www.blackrosewriting.com

Printed in the United States of America
Suggested Retail Price (SRP) $22.95

Dreamer on the Mountain is printed in Garamond

*As a planet-friendly publisher, Black Rose Writing does its best to eliminate
unnecessary waste to reduce paper usage and energy costs, while never
compromising the reading experience. As a result, the final word count vs. page
count may not meet common expectations.